The

VIADUCT

Doubleday

NEW YORK LONDON TORONTO

SYDNEY AUCKLAND

The
Viaduct

A HARLEM THRILLER

Grace F. Edwards

PUBLISHED BY DOUBLEDAY
a division of Random House, Inc.

DOUBLEDAY and the portrayal of an anchor
with a dolphin are registered
trademarks of Random House, Inc.

Book design by Dana Leigh Treglia

Library of Congress Cataloging-in-Publication Data
Edwards, Grace F. (Grace Frederica)
The viaduct : a Harlem thriller / Grace F. Edwards.
— 1st ed.
p. cm.
1. Harlem (New York, N.Y.)—Fiction.   2. African
Americans—Fiction.   I. Title.
PS3555.D99V3 2003
813'.54—dc21
2003046277

ISBN 0-385-50200-1

PRINTED IN THE UNITED STATES OF AMERICA

January 2004
First Edition

1   3   5   7   9   10   8   6   4   2

FOR PERRI AND SIMONE

AND THE HARLEM WRITERS GUILD

The

VIADUCT

CHAPTER 1

Harlem, August 1972

Marin eased off the bar stool and walked over to the jukebox, dropped a quarter, and randomly pressed five selections. The music was older than the box and held no surprises but most of the patrons who hung out in the Fat Man Bar rarely complained.

Even the brothers who attended the lodge meetings a few doors away felt a certain comfort in the familiar sounds of Hadda Brooks and Ella Johnson. Marin had once toyed with the idea of joining the lodge so that when the regular Thursday night meetings ended and the members crowded into the Fat Man, he wouldn't feel so left out. Not that their conversations were exclusive, but at those times he'd been the only one in the place, other than the bartender, not wearing a business suit.

Tonight the place was empty. Without the press of bodies to absorb it, the music echoed off the dim-lit mocha-tinted walls and hung heavy in the air, blending with the faintly stale smell of cigarettes and wet glasses draining on damp towels. The dark oak of the bar was polished to a sheen that appeared almost wet, like a stream of water had flowed down its length and had never dried.

If Marin leaned over, as he sometimes did when he had a lot on his mind, he could catch his reflection perfectly in the low spark of the frosted lamplight. His hair was cut close against an unremarkable face and he rarely smiled. When he did, the shadow in his eyes dissipated and a deep brown patina complemented his smooth skin.

He wheeled slowly on the stool again, pushed away from the railing, and strolled to the wall phone near the entrance to the men's room. He checked his watch as he dialed, listened to the distant buzz, then to Margaret's low voice.

"Hello?"

"Margaret? How you doin'?"

"Marin? Honey, where are you? I was about to put dinner on the table . . ."

Marin stared at the wall in front of him. Up close, he could make out the dull beige streaks mixed in with the brown. He did not want to tell Margaret that he had stopped by the Fat Man; that something had happened to make him detour for a beer and a chance to get his thoughts together before facing her. Besides, the Fat Man was where Chancey, loud and belligerent Chancey, hung out. He'd brought him home to meet Margaret. Once. And Chancey'd found fault with nearly everything. Not in so many words, but in his hard, nervous stare.

He had invited him to dinner, and after, they had stepped out into the dim hallway—because Margaret didn't like the smell of cigarettes in the apartment.

Chance inhaled, held it for a second, then allowed the smoke to drift in a spiral toward the courtyard window. He leaned near the bannister and Marin sat on the marble steps, watching him, listening to the faint noise of James Brown drifting from a radio on the floor below. He wanted to smoke but, mindful of his three-a-day limit, decided to wait. He could always come back out later.

Chance took another drag, long and slow so that the tip glowed like a dot of coal in the hall. "You lucky, man. You real lucky."

Marin leaned back against the step, waiting.

"I mean your wife. This the first time I seen her, 'cept for them pictures you showed me in 'Nam. She's beautiful. Like somethin' out of the movies, man."

The cigarette had burned down and he flicked the stub through the window into the backyard. "Thanks for dinner, my man. I got to get goin'."

"She made dessert."

"Nah. Can't stay. Thanks anyway . . ."

Marin had known Chance from his army days and understood what Vietnam had done to both of them. When they returned home, he understood what it was like for a man to work, and on bad days, challenge anyone including his supervisor to approach him.

They had finally given Chance a street route delivering mail in the toughest blocks in Harlem, and he took the assignment as if he had been waiting for it all his life.

Still, Marin wondered what it must be like to have a sizable bank balance yet live in a small room with only the noise of television to keep him company; to not have his own stove, or someone to eat and sleep with and help soften the edge of memory. The main reason why, Marin thought, Chance spent so much time at the lodge and in the bar.

Marin held the phone to his ear, his attention divided as Margaret spoke. He knew that once he told her where he was, she usually softened and he was able to hang out longer. Telling her made her relax, and he didn't have to worry about rushing home.

But tonight was different. Why was he hanging out? He should have gotten off the subway at 145th Street, moved on down the hill past all the music and mayhem in the Brown Bomber Bar, and gone straight home.

But he had allowed the doors of the A train to close in his face and open again one stop farther, where he stepped off at 155th Street and strolled into the Fat Man.

He tried not to think about why he did it and concentrated instead on Margaret. Something in her voice, low and serene, calmed him, made him ask, "What's on the menu?"

"Pot roast. And I think I got it right this time . . . "

Marin's heart sank. Margaret was a good cook but when she failed at something, she was determined to keep at it until she got it right. Pot roast was one of those things. She could spend a hundred dollars on eye round, and somewhere between the meat market and his dinner plate, it would transform itself into the toughest slice of leather he'd ever seen.

"Uh, sounds good. What else we havin' with it?" Maybe he could fill up on the rice and gravy, a heavy salad, and a beer.

"Potatoes and green peas and . . . Listen Marin, I know what you're thinkin' but this time it came out right. The only thing is, I don't want to overcook it . . . I—"

"Okay. Okay, baby. Be right there."

Maybe after dinner he'd be able to tell her what had happened.

He hung up the phone. Jimmy, the bartender, was stacking glasses on the shelves, his back to the bar. Marin was not sure if he had overheard the conversation and was glad he hadn't mentioned anything to Margaret. Time enough to tell her face-to-face.

"Listen, Jimmy. Tell Chance I'll catch 'im later. I just remembered I'm supposed to pick up some ice cream for Margaret. Catch the store before it close . . ."

Jimmy turned around and rang up fifty cents for Marin's beer.

"How's Margaret doin'? Still enjoyin' that butter pecan?"

"Every day, practically. Lately she been mixin' it with a little strawberry though . . . gotta pick up some now . . ."

Jimmy wanted to say that there was nothing like variety but he knew how touchy some guys felt about their queens, especially when they were expecting their first baby. He wanted to tell him that she looked even prettier with those few extra pounds but decided to keep his mouth closed.

Instead, he glanced at the large clock on the wall. It was shaped like an octagon with RHEINGOLD BEER scripted in neon letters around the numbers.

"Some kind of special committee meetin' tonight. Probably be over in another ten, fifteen minutes," he noted.

Marin wanted to tell him about the pot roast but shook his head and remained silent. He knew from Jimmy's size and conversation that he was a chittlin snacker from way back and would only laugh at his predicament. He could hear him now. "Naw. Margaret sure ain't no Carolina gal. Carolina gal cook anything under the sun ain't breathin' and can fit in a pot . . . And cook it right!"

It was easier, Marin felt, to talk about ice cream. Even the other problem had faded momentarily.

"Gotta pick up some before the store closes," he said again. "Tell Chance I catch him later, tomorrow, maybe, before the last figure."

"Be cool."

He headed for the door as the sounds of the Cats and The Fiddle slid from the mesh-covered grill of the jukebox, the voices calling like young boys, high and earnest against the background of metallic chords:

. . . Now you're so fine . . . And I love you so . . .

The sound was almost enough to make Marin change his mind, stay, and see what else was coming up on the box.

"Ain't that something, Jimmy? They cut that way, way before I was born and it still sound good. I remember my folks movin' to the groove."

"Yeah, that's the real thing. They ain't makin' 'em like they used to. But them new kids, the Jackson Five? They got stuff goin' on. Come on the scene and took it over. Big time."

A minute later, Marin closed the door on the heavy guitar sounds. The night heat hit him in the face and he unbuttoned his shirt collar as he strolled across St. Nicholas Avenue. He thought of Chance, who worked overtime, and how he had urged Marin to try for the job.

"Pay's good. And ain't nobody bother you. That's what I like. Nobody bother me." But no, I liked where I was. The print shop was small but folks didn't bother you there either. Boss was all right. Bonus every Christmas the last couple years. Didn't need nothing like the post office where you only a name, maybe a number. Like the army. Had enough of that shit. Besides, I probably couldn't lift no mail bags anyway. 'Nam seen to that. Back ain't worth nuthin' . . .

But maybe I shoulda listened. Took a gamble. Now I'm out. Boss had a second heart attack. Damn kids don't want no part of the business so he packed it in. Movin' to Florida and I'm movin' to unemployment. Place close up tight right after lunch and I'm out of a job. Better enjoy this pot roast. Long time before we see another one.

The light changed as he crossed the street but he did not rush.

Tonight his back was acting up and his steps were small and deliberate and lent a fluid movement to his tall, thin frame. He walked toward the viaduct, a decaying gray steel-and-stone structure that rose ten stories above Eighth Avenue and stretched from St. Nicholas to Seventh Avenue.

Marin strolled down the walkway, leaving the tall, elegant buildings of Sugar Hill behind.

Now he glanced over the railing at the patched and tarred rooftops of the five-story tenements that lined the street below. On a good day in winter, he could see all the way over to the Harlem River but now the view was obscured by the hundred-year-old Norway maples that lined Seventh Avenue. They stood like ancient sentries with gnarled arms, impotent in the face of the creeping neglect that defined the neighborhood.

. . . Lindsay tryin' hard but that urban renewal stuff just ain't happenin' fast enough.

He lit a cigarette and continued down the slight incline.

. . . Still warm but no rain, thank God. Last coupla nights was hell. No matter how hot it gets, Margaret gotta wrap up like a mummy. Blanket head to toe like she keepin' the baby warm. And it ain't even here yet.

He thought of her and the baby, the pot roast, the prospect of finding another job, and he slowed down. The half-light lingering from the day's scorching sun had disappeared quick and quiet, as if a shade had come down to bathe the path in a blue darkness.

There was no one in sight and the echo of his footfalls was loud in the silence.

Used to run down this thing in three seconds flat when I was a kid. Wasn't smokin' then. Feet didn't touch the ground. That was then. Gotta give these smokes up. Still in shape for thirty, even with my back out sometimes.

He walked leisurely, surprised that he was alone but enjoying the solitude. He gazed beyond the junction where the viaduct ended and the bridge began. Beyond the bridge, over the Harlem River, Yankee Stadium loomed large, silent, and empty.

Playin' Boston . . . If things was different, I coulda stayed in the bar and caught what's left of it on the box.

He remembered that the television was broken, hanging over the long bar in mid-ceiling for weeks now, big, abstract, and empty while the owner debated whether to have it repaired or replaced.

Better make up his mind. Series be here before he know it. That's another thing I wanted to get. Promised Margaret she'd have a TV before the baby comes. Flip Wilson's on for a whole hour. First black show since they took Nat Cole off. I guess that's what the Man calls progress. And Margaret could've—

"Say, my man, you got a match?"

Marin stopped. Two strangers—one squat, bold, with arms roped with muscles; the other tall, thin, and nervous—had sidled up to him. They wore white straw wide-brim hats, the lids broken low under the crowns. He had not even heard them until they approached. They had come up the stairs from Eighth Avenue. That exit had been closed for years because some steps had collapsed. Two rough boards nailed in the shape of a wide X had been in place for so long that people passed by without thinking of it.

He had not thought of it either and now here they were, on a Friday, somebody's payday, when everyone knew that *match* was another word for *money.*

Quickly he said, "Can't help you 'cause I ain't got it!"

He made a move and they crowded him, easing on either side, pretending to join him in his stroll.

The muscular one spoke and his voice floated like a whisper on the night air, but underneath Marin caught the shade of violence.

"Since you ain't got no match, you got to have somethin' . . ."

"Nuthin' you want," Marin said. He turned to the thin one, then glanced back to see if anyone else might be on the walkway. It was empty. A bus sped by noisily, its bright-lit windows catching the three men in a brief moving spotlight.

Marin held his breath, hoping that it would stop at the end of the viaduct and discharge at least one passenger. Instead, it slowed, then made a sharp right turn onto Seventh Avenue and was gone.

Then the thin one spoke. "Les' see what this sucka got . . ." His words spilled out, hissing like air suddenly blown out of a tire.

Marin kept walking. "Listen, man! I just got laid off. Lost my jay-oh-bee. I oughtta be snakin' you."

He could feel their shoulders touch him as they walked. He imagined he smelled the sharp, rank odor of sweat and knew it did not belong to him but to the thin one who moved beside him, jerking like a broken-stringed marionette. Marin glanced at him and then looked straight ahead, amazed that he was more angry than afraid.

They seemed to walk faster; then suddenly the two stopped and blocked him and he noticed for the first time that under the wide brims they had thin, dark stockings stretched over their faces.

"Don't make no funny moves and everything be okay. Les' see your stash—"

"Aw no, motherfucka! Come at me and you be talkin' out the side of your neck!"

The muscular one hit Marin in the stomach so hard the jab took his breath away. He sank to his knees and just avoided a blow to the back of his head. He grabbed the legs of the muscular man and brought him down on the ground, determined to kill him. No one had ever hit him like that in his life, not even in basic training, not even hand-to-hand in the knee-deep stinking mud of the Mekong Delta.

Marin rolled on the ground and managed to tear through the net, to get his fingers into the man's eyes, all the while trying to shake off the light blows of the thin man bobbing and weaving around them like a referee.

The street lamp was broken and they struggled on the dark sidewalk. Marin's throat was hoarse with rage. "I'm-a kill you, motherfucka, I'm-a kill you . . ."

He was able to get to his feet, dragging the man up with him. They grappled and stumbled against the guardrail and Marin suddenly swooped down, gripped the man by his ankles and propelled him over the rail to the street ten stories below.

He turned in a low crouch to face the second one but was out of breath, out of step, and the knife was in him before he saw it. He held up his hand but the thin one was too fast. The knife came down a second time with the impact of a hammer dropped on his chest. The man's hat flew off, sailed away over the railing and into the wind, and the shrouded face howled even as his hand went through Marin's pocket.

Everything happened so fast. Marin's shirt felt sticky and he began to stagger, to run from the other sounds boiling up like smoke from the crowd gathering in the street below.

But something arced up his spine, eclipsing the sharp agony in his chest. He sank to the pavement and saw the thin man running away and wondered why he could not hear his footsteps. Even the noise of the gathering crowd below was lost in a strange sound filling his ears.

It was the crashing break of a wave hitting the beach. He could hear it coming at him as he struggled to stay ahead of it and hold his rifle above his shoulders and balance the backpack. The wet earth shifted beneath his feet as the force of the wave drew the sandy water out into the wide river to double back and hit him again and bear him down into its lightless center.

He opened one eye to see a car pass, skid to a halt, then back up. Its doors slammed open and several people jumped out. Voices merged with the breaking wave.

"Oh, shit! Lookit that!"

"He need an ambulance!"

"Naw. Can't wait. He losin' blood by the gallon!"

By now, the pain that had flashed through his chest and back and stomach was gone. He thought he heard Chance's voice but it faded to silence. He felt only the press of the wave, warm and seductive, pulling against him and he wished he could lie back and relax.

A hand was under his head, trying to lift him up, to cradle him as he struggled to get a word past the hot liquid bubbling up in his throat. He heard:

"What's your name? Can you talk? You know the cat that knifed you?"

Another voice: "Pocket's inside out. Probably robbery. We saw him runnin' away. Hang on, man. Hang on . . ."

. . . Hang on . . . to . . . what? What is there to hang on to when wave after wave is pounding your back and chest and stomach and you're so tired you no longer feel your legs in the water. The rifle was gone, sunk like a stone in the muck. Hang on to a . . . froth of bubbles, a bit . . . of seaweed . . . a star . . .

His thoughts raced, scattered, then collided.

He had seen a star. Once, when he had been high and making love to Margaret, a small speck, glowing orange, had shot across his line of vision, blurring the sight of her parted mouth, and frightening him nearly to death, but not enough to make him stop until he had finished what she had started. He had lain on the wet sheets and wondered if any other woman could have made that happen.

He opened his eyes again and made a monumental effort to break through the liquid that glued his tongue to the roof of his mouth. The sound pushed above the roar to the listening ear.

"Margaret. Tell Margaret . . ."

"What's your name, man? What's your name?"

"Marin . . . Taylor. Tell Margaret I . . ."

But the wave came again, hitting with a force that made him forget what it was he wanted to say. Maybe it was about the star. He had never told her. He had been too frightened at the time. Or maybe it was the ice cream. Or the roast. That was it.

"Tell Margaret I love her. You tell her Marin said . . ."

"Hold on, man, you gonna tell her yourself. You gonna make it."

He felt he was floating but he was being lifted and someone from far away said, "What we waitin' for? We got to hustle!"

CHAPTER 2

*T*he fist on the door was loud and sudden and caused Margaret to drop the spoon she was about to place near Marin's plate. She had expected to hear his key in the door, not this loud banging. She stepped back and stared.

. . . Dropped a spoon. Bad news comin'. Mr. Bowen's dog howling all last night like it seen somethin'. Now a spoon dropped. From my table. Lord help me . . .

The bell rang and the fist pounded again and she called out from where she stood.

"Who is it?"

"Police. We have to talk to a Mrs. Taylor."

Margaret's gaze wandered from the spoon to the small space in the foyer. Yes, that was her name. She put her hands to her face and wondered why it was necessary to open the door.

The two policemen wore the official mask appropriate for certain occasions. In the awkward silence, one coughed lightly, and somewhere over his shoulder, Margaret heard the small click of her neighbor's door. Then the older officer spoke.

"Mrs. Taylor, your husband's been involved in an incident. He's—"

Margaret held out her hand to push the next words away.

"No!" she said firmly, thinking of the spoon. Then something, a weight, descended and came to rest on her shoulder.

"No," she said again. Softly.

"You have to come to the hospital."

She did not respond immediately, and the three of them stood silently in the small foyer with the hard overhead light that she hated and that Marin had promised to replace.

The tiny naked bulb bathed them in sharp relief as they stood, Margaret as still as stone and the two policemen shifting from one foot to the other, wondering how long they would have to be there, hoping the woman standing in the door wouldn't go into sudden labor at the news.

"Uh . . . you'd better hurry . . . is there somone who could come with you . . . if you feel . . . ?"

She looked in the direction of the voice. It was the younger cop speaking, and clearly less experienced in coping with someone else's grief. She stared at him, wanting to roll his words up and place them like a dry tablet on the back of his tongue where it would be easy for him to swallow, but instead more and more sounds pushed forward through lips that barely seemed to part.

"We not sure. Might've been robbery . . . not sure."

Margaret turned from them to look past the fallen spoon to the small dining table, the two plates, napkins, glasses, and one incomplete silver setting. At the end of the table, Marin's old shirt hung carelessly across the chair. She had forgotten to remove it that morning.

Don't call anybody. Mama would get too upset. Sister just as bad. I'll call 'em after I see what's what. It can't be that bad. It can't be.

When she finally spoke, her voice was quiet in the stillness.

"No," she said to no one in particular. "I'll go by myself. There's been a mistake. I know it."

She picked up the shirt and folded it over her arm. "He'll need this," she said again to no one in particular. "He'll need a shirt."

CHAPTER 3

*M*argaret sat on a small iron chair next to the bed listening to Marin's ragged breathing. It had been five days since he'd been transferred from intensive care. Now he shared a room with three other patients. One man was on a respirator, another appeared to be sleeping, his head encased in a cocoon of plaster, and the third, an old man with a wide, gaping mouth, lay on his side staring at the ceiling and murmuring something Margaret could not understand.

Other, louder sounds moved around her but she sat, too terrified to speak, afraid she'd miss the moment when Marin might stop breathing. His face was still swollen, his upper lip was split, and the left eye was rimmed in purple. His chest was a small hill of bandages that rose and fell and she clocked the movements, timed them, to make certain that one intake lasted no longer, no deeper, than the one before.

She blocked out everything else, ignored Marin's friend Chance, reduced his scowling presence to a meaningless shadow hovering near the foot of the bed.

Occasionally, Chance's voice broke through, but it was a sound she did not want to hear. "How in hell could somethin' like this happen? After all the shi—stuff we been through, he come home and have somethin' like this go down? Don't make no sense. Don't make no sense!"

It made no sense. When she had called her mother and sister, there were screams and tears but no answers either. They had rushed to the hospital and cried some more, then worried about what was going to happen to her. If he died, she'd be without a husband and struggling to bring up a child all alone. If he survived, surely he could not work again, at least for a long time.

No one had answers and so she ignored everyone, pretended not to hear when someone said, "If he come in squawkin', guaranteed he'll go out walkin'."

It was Chance's cigarette voice. Her mother had leaned up from over Marin's bed and stared at Chance as if he had told a bad joke at a bad time. That was two days ago, and now he was back again to continue his restless pacing.

"Don't make no sense . . ."

Margaret ignored him and concentrated on the sight and slow rhythm of Marin's chest. Her mouth moved but the words stayed inside.

. . . He's gotta live to see his baby. Live, even if he's paralyzed, can't walk, can't sit up, can't work anymore. Just let him live. Let him live. I will take care of him.

CHAPTER 4

"*T*he guy on the pavement had a shredded stocking looped around his neck. Did you know him?"

Marin looked at the two men. The black guy's face was shaped like a burnt puff pastry and his neck overflowed the collar of his pinstripe shirt. He removed his hat and introduced himself as Detective Eddie Benjamin, and Marin saw that his hair was cut in a modified Afro—thick enough to satisfy the brothers on the beat and short enough to avoid panic in the precinct. His tie, yellow silk dotted with images of tiny kittens, was knotted tight enough to cut off the limited air circulating in the small space between him and Marin.

The other man, tall and rangy with a lined face and thin yellow hair, stood behind Benjamin. He said nothing but flashed his badge and smiled pleasantly. Marin could not see his name but his watery blue eyes reminded him of a ghost.

Marin lay back on the pillow to put some distance between them but Detective Benjamin moved closer, repositioning his small notepad on one knee and tilting his straw hat on the other. His dark face was wet with the August heat.

"They tried to rob me," Marin finally said.

Benjamin nodded and scribbled something. "Okay. Robbery. How did he go over the side?"

"He fell. We fought and he tripped and flipped and his buddy skipped. Left me crawlin' in my own blood."

Benjamin took his time. He wrote almost a paragraph and Marin looked around the room as he waited. The other detective seemed to follow his gaze.

There were three beds. Two men were asleep but the man on the respirator was gone and the mattress was now rolled up.

The windows were bare of curtains and the ceiling had a faint spidery pattern of cracks radiating from the brass light fixture. The light was off and the sun's rays slanted pale yellow through the window and across the bed.

Marin's breath slowed. He was in a hospital. He was not staring up at a hole in a camouflaged makeshift ceiling, listening to the roar of M-16s and the screams of dying men. He was not lying in mud and blood, waiting for the medic to stumble over the bodies, then yell, "This one's breathing. Don't tag 'im," before kneeling with the syringe.

There was no whistle of the near-miss, no breath held waiting for the earth to settle again before the medic drew the plunger back to pump a shot that sailed him temporarily into another universe.

This room was quiet. Clean. Only Detective Benjamin and his ghostly partner were there. Benjamin had stopped writing, held his pen at an angle over the notebook, and was looking at him.

"Mr. Taylor? You all right?"

"Yeah. Sorry. What was it you said?"

"I wanted to know if you'd be able to recognize the one who got away?"

"I don't think so. They had those stockings or something over their faces. All I know is that one, the one that went over, was kind of short with plenty of muscle. The other guy was skinny. And kinda jumpy. Like he mighta been on drugs."

The other detective spoke up: "That's what we need to know, Taylor. Was this a deal gone bad?"

Marin stared at him. "What the fuck kinda question is that? Listen, I was robbed of my pay. My wallet had an envelope with four weeks severence in it. What the hell are you talkin' about?"

A flash of pain made him close his eyes. He held his breath, waiting for it to fade. When he was able to focus again, he saw Benjamin glancing at his partner; then he coughed a light cough and snapped his notebook closed.

"Okay, Mr. Taylor. Didn't mean to wear you out. Probably drop by tomorrow. The day after, maybe."

Benjamin rose and moved away from the bed. He was six feet three and his bulky frame crowded the door but he was light on his feet and almost seemed to glide past the nurse's station in the center of the corridor. His partner lingered at the door and before he disappeared he scanned Marin's face as if to remember it.

Margaret walked in and paused to stare at his retreating back. "Who was that?"

"I didn't get his name but he's Detective Benjamin's partner. Playin' that tired old good-cop bad-cop shi—stuff. They're askin' questions I can't answer. Second time they been here."

He looked at her and his mind rolled away from the incident. "How you doin', baby?"

"Okay." She smiled to hide her apprehension.

She pulled back the cover and helped him out of bed. His back felt like a board but yesterday he had been able to sit up, wave away the painkillers, and walk a few steps. Today he made it to the window to gaze out on the crowd moving along Lenox Avenue and 135th Street.

People emerged from the subway and walked the few steps to Pan-Pan's restaurant. Vendors hawked their wares—everything from transistor batteries, straw hats, bean pies, and newspapers to fresh fruit. He watched a troop of Girl Scouts enter the Schomburg Center. They moved through the door and he wondered about the new exhibit. The photos in the window were too far away for him to make out the details.

Marin had for days drifted in and out of consciousness, and when he was able to focus, it seemed as if a season had come and gone. Now he turned from the window to look again at Margaret. He saw a face dark brown beautiful with eyes large and as expressive as her smile. Her braids were wrapped around her head like a halo. Her stomach was big, and she was still ready to reach for his hand, prop him up, feed him, even though he could now do that himself.

He placed his hand on her stomach and spread his fingers wide. "I can feel it. The baby's moving, getting impatient."

Margaret smiled and slid his hand away. "Not here. Suppose somebody comes in."

"So what?" He leaned forward and kissed her. "It's been awhile. God, I miss you, baby."

"When can you come home?"

"I don't know. Probably another week. I guess the doctor wants to make sure everything's back in the right place."

"So do I. I love you, Marin."

She leaned forward and pressed her head into his shoulder. He closed his eyes and breathed in the scent of her hair pomade.

"I love you too, baby."

He heard the soft sound of her breathing and wondered how he would cope if anything were to happen to her. He'd heard vague stories of things happening to some women during delivery. Suppose, because of the baby, something . . .

He opened his eyes. His voice was mellow when he spoke. "Probably by the time I'm ready to come home, you'll be ready to come in. Time's nearly here."

"I know. I can't wait. These extra pounds are getting to me."

"Won't be long now, baby. Won't be long."

He held her face between his hands and then smoothed her hair. "Listen, I can feel you tightenin' up. You worried about somethin'? Ain't nuthin' to worry about. The worst is over. You and the baby'll be home and I'll be out of here, able to look for another job and . . ."

"Another job?" Margaret stepped back, her hand to her mouth. "What happened to . . . ? No wonder, I got no answer when I called the shop. I wanted them to know that you— Oh, Marin. What happened?"

He closed his eyes again, remembering now what he had not told her. "Listen, baby. The old man got sick and the place closed. Everybody got a pink ticket. Not just me. But soon as I'm able, I'll find something else. I learned the printing business from A to Z. Maybe open my own place. We gonna be fine, baby. Fine."

She buried her face in his shoulder and held her breath. She wished he could leave the hospital right now. Today. And get well at home. Something was happening that she couldn't put her finger on.

She was good at signs but some things had been happening since he had been in the hospital.

I don't want to add another worry for him. What good would it do? He is where he is and I am where I am. But I can't ignore those sounds, almost like rat sounds, like something or somebody scratching at the door.

I have to manage. Just have to, at least till he's back home. Between Mama and my sister running in and out checking on me, it's not too bad. They want me to spend the time till Marin comes home with them but what would I look like runnin' from my own house, scared of every creak and crack come my way? No.

She leaned into Marin carefully so as not to hurt him.

I'll just keep the radio low so I can hear. Sharpen that kitchen knife to a thin edge and keep it near the door when that noise comes again.

CHAPTER 5

*C*onroy skirted the pile of garbage lining the curb and made his way down the block. A fast-moving bank of clouds scudded across the moon, blanking it, and this made him feel better. He walked softly on the balls of his feet, ignoring the dim lights of Lenox Avenue shimmering in the distance. He moved along the unbroken row of five-story tenements, scanning scarred doors and the darkened hallways beyond, listening for the slightest sound.

For the last two weeks, he had had to hole up in Sadie's place, listen to her run her mouth nonstop about the fix he had gotten himself into, and how she could get herself another man or do bad all by herself if he didn't straighten up soon.

Half the time, he had ignored her, told himself he could always get another woman. Reminded himself he wasn't half bad-looking except for that zigzag tattoo on his eyebrow left over from a bar fight. Light stuff. Scar only meant he'd had to walk with his blade from then on. Light stuff. Scar or not, his close-cut hair, keen features, and otherwise smooth brown skin had been his passport into so many beds he'd stopped counting long ago and he was not yet thirty. So she could holler all she wanted.

Mostly, he spent the time thinking of his dead brother and knew that it wasn't worth going anywhere until the heat cooled. *Take it easy and let her holler.*

He had to steer clear of the streets, especially Seventh Avenue, with the club and lounge lights blinking holiday bright around the windows—except it was August and no holiday in sight.

The block was dark, and he tried to stroll nonchalantly, glancing around only occasionally to make certain he was alone. Except for the dry skitter of rats raiding the garbage at the curb, the street was silent. He took off his straw hat and wiped at the sweat gathered across his forehead. His shirt stuck to his skin as he moved and he wondered what story he was going to tell when he reached the house at the end of the block. Nothing seemed real. What was he going to say to his mother?

. . . *Tito's gone. Gone, damn it. Shit happened so fast. How was we supposed to know. Dude tippin' so funny-like. We pinned him, thought he was some kinda easy sissy, way he walked. But motherfucka turned and kicked ass. Tito's dead. I couldn't even show my face at his funeral. Had to lay low. What the fuck is this? And now I can't even stroll the strip for a while. Got to keep my shit low. Ain't this a bitch!*

Before everything changed, he used to enjoy standing with his brother, waiting in the shadows on the strip—eyeing all the big places. One Friday, it might be Smalls' Paradise. The next weekend, maybe Basie's Lounge. And Mr. B's with that canopy stretching to the curb. He especially liked when the action up the avenue heated up. When Adam Clayton Powell and his politician pals strolled into the Red Rooster, they acted like they owned not just the space but the whole world. And in a way, they did. Pullin' on those big cigars and champagne poppin' all over the place. And when the crowd got too tight in the Rooster, Jock's Place, right upstairs, caught the spillover.

. . . *High-class stops where top-down Caddies and Buick Deuce 'n' a Quarters pulled to the curb. Money men behind the wheel with women so fine, you get arrested just for stealin' a glance.*

He liked watching, but to Tito, Friday night was money. Sometimes, during the week, when they'd run short and have to go out again, he liked that even better, liked feeling the tension uncoil like a rope in his stomach as they waited, and liked the way his lungs enlarged and hit hard against his rib cage as if he had just won a race.

In another world, the mayor, tall and good-looking, had brought a touch of class to Gracie Mansion and set about proclaiming, "New York is Fun City."

The *Amsterdam* liked his style, and through Har-You Act and other million-dollar antipoverty programs, he further endeared himself to the folks uptown. The new Harlem Hospital building had recently opened. *Harlem on My Mind* was exhibiting at the Metropolitan Museum of Art, and Barbara Ann Teer's National Black Theatre opened.

A few years earlier, at a block party on 139th Street, Jimi Hendrix had performed with Maxine Brown, Big Maybelle, and the LaRoque Bey dancers, and after the performance Jimi had announced to a wildly cheering crowd that he had "finally come home," affirming that New York was indeed Fun City.

But in the uncompromising light of day, Harlem reflected its own reality: The old 1950s urban renewal blueprint meant razing historic structures and erecting massive and sterile housing projects. It meant forced relocation rather than renewal. Four units were destroyed for one unit of low-cost housing, and entire blocks of turn-of-the-century brownstones became a memory.

The remnants of the blueprint were visible in the neglected tenements, school buildings that mimicked ancient ruins, rows of abandoned stores with steel shutters coated with graffiti, and churches battling to contain the devastation and shore up dwindling congregations.

James Foreman of SNCC interrupted Sunday services at Riverside Church to present a "Black Manifesto" to a surprised congregation. He demanded support for black economic development from white Christian churches, Jewish synagogues, all part and parcel of the capitalist system, and demanded that they begin to pay five hundred million dollars in reparations.

A Rand Corporation study urged the city to turn over slum properties to black tenants to end the reign of white landlords. No one listened. Folks who were able scraped together a two- or three-thousand-dollar down payment and fled to new homes in the suburbs. Those who remained fought to stay a step ahead of any accident of fate that might pull them deeper into their misery. And as a coda, the White Plague—heroin—howled across the terrain like a blizzard, crippling the inhabitants, burying in its drifts those who thought they could handle a little one-on-one. It accentuated the decay and daylight burned into the senses like fire.

Night was different. A cloak fell and darkness smoked the lenses. The hard edge faded and the other side of Harlem shimmered like carefully applied lip gloss. Music was the language of night and the smile of the partygoers was reflected in the glow of club lights. Laughter echoed down the strip and died only when the sun showed its face again.

. . . No night was slow. We pinned not only the clubs but a lot of the hangout spots too: the Rennie Lounge, the Peacock, William's Tavern, the Embassy. Tito was right. No tellin' who might be wheelin' out. Specially 'round three when the lights got low.

All we did was wait and watch. Somethin' fall right in our lap. Didn't have to do nuthin'.

. . . That was the way it was. We knew the deal. Could hang for hours and it always worked. Track and attack. Wasn't our fault chump ain't know when to skip that last taste. We ain't forced him to pick up that last glass. One for the road, Tito always said, was the one trip their ass up. And it worked like straight up magic till two weeks ago. Motherfucker had to go jump bad. Wouldn't give it up. Shanked 'im but I was too damn slow. Now Tito gone. And where I'm at? What I'm gonna do? My main man's gone.

He walked more slowly, thinking of his brother, the older, smarter one who had studied all the angles and found a way to make it pay. Tito showed him how he could always have some dollars in his pocket without breaking a sweat. Maybe not as much as the money men styling back behind the wheels of those fine cars. Those were guys dressed in clothes that would cost him and Tito a year's pay. If they were working. But everybody couldn't sweat the same. Why should they? There were always other games.

And so their hunter's eyes followed the money, the partygoers who strolled from the cars into the bars, and those who came on foot. They listened to the jazz and blues notes float in the air as the doors opened and closed. Then they waited. Patiently. Until someone stepped out again, alone. Nighttime was the right time.

One slow night as they waited with no prospects in sight, Tito had passed the time planning what they would do if they ever had a big score: They'd lay low for a while, then one night maybe step into one of the clubs. Lean on the bar like the money men, or better yet, catch the first thing smoking to Las Vegas. It was a dream that made them laugh.

Three houses away from the corner of Lenox Avenue, he slowed again to glance in back of him. The streetlight was so dim he could not make out his own shadow. The stealthy echo of his footsteps followed him and he was glad for the sound.

Most of the buildings had been boarded up, and few people walked through the block. Even so, he had to be careful. The street was still empty. The house facing him was as dark as the others and he climbed the broken steps quickly and slipped inside.

The lobby was even darker but the stairs leading to the third floor were illuminated by the streetlight slanting through the window. He waded through boxes and bags stacked on the landings and nearly slipped when something stuck to his foot.

"Damn!"

He leaned against the wall, scraped his shoe on the edge of the step, then moved faster, as if he had already wasted too much time.

I'll be in and out. Let her know what's goin' on. What I'm gonna do.

Of the four apartments on the floor, three were sealed. He approached the door of the unsealed one and knocked once, then waited a breath before he rapped again, three times in quick, light succession. He listened in the dark to the dull scrape of the piece of two-by-four being lifted from the iron hasps. Then the door creaked open.

His mother cupped her hand over a candle burning in a small mayonnaise jar and stared at him in the wavering light.

"Conroy! I thought you was back in jail!"

"Naw. Naw. I'm here. Ran into some static but I'm here."

He eased inside and watched his mother close the door and slam the wood bar back through the hasps.

"This is your fault," she said, her back to him. When she turned, he saw the tears about to spill.

"This is your fault," she whispered again. "I know it is. Don't tell me nuthin'. Junior wouldn't been in no trouble if you hadn't put him up to it. If it wasn't for you, he'd still be here."

Her voice, thickened by fatigue, was barely a whisper as she moved past him, holding to the wall to steady herself. Conroy noticed that her limp had gotten a lot worse from the time he had last seen her. He followed her down the narrow hall, stumbling in the dark over unfamiliar junk.

In a large room overlooking the street, more candles cast a brighter orange glow and he was able to see her face more clearly. She leaned against the wall away from him and he saw that her skin had taken on the color and texture of dry leaves.

He felt tired and wanted to sit down but there was no place except on a packing box. He eased down and waited, knowing that she was also waiting, wanting to hear what he had to say, and maybe for him to trip himself in the telling.

"Ma, look. It ain't the way you think. It didn't happen the way you heard."

"How you know what I heard?"

"Uh, well. I don't, but stuff got a way of gettin' 'round and some-time words get lost in the tellin'. You know, they fall between the commas?"

She gazed at him, ignoring his weak attempt at humor. A minute passed and he heard her sigh.

She moved to sit on a box facing him, had to ease down, and he thought he heard small bones snap in the silence.

"Okay now," she said again. "Suppose we talk sense. What happened? How Tito get to fall off the viaduct? Smash so bad, casket couldn't be open. And how come you couldn't even show up at the funeral? That's why I thought you didn't show. They was holdin' you on somethin'."

Conroy peered around him, then looked out of the window, trying to frame his words. Everything he planned to say had gone out of his head. He didn't know what he was going to do. He and Tito had talked of moving her out of this place. But where?

Con Edison had cut the electricity when the building had been condemned to make way for new housing that never happened.

Of the twenty families, eight had nowhere to go, four others recognized a freebie when they saw one, and all in all, about a dozen, including his mother, had moved back in. In winter, the reek of kerosene could be smelled down the block. In the summer, the smell of garbage was worse. Two years. He and Tito were supposed to get her out of here long ago.

Instead, Tito had hooked a light from the street to her place but someone else, either above or below, had cut it and stolen it. Now all she had were the candles.

. . . We was supposed to get her out, me and him. But so much other shit had got in the way. First there was the little problem of kicking H. Tito had come back from Dannemora clean, lookin' like he had muscles in his toenails, and sayin' there was no point in throwin' dollars after a dream you could never catch up to.

Instead of talking me out of my habit—which he coulda done—he had me locked in a room. Motherfucker locked me up and kept the key in his pocket. Threw in some eats and water from time to time and, for I don't remember how long, pretended he didn't know me, didn't hear me screamin' and bangin' a hole in the walls with my head and rollin' in my own shit till there was nothin' left, then draggin' me out and into that damn tub of ice water.

And all he had to say was, "From now on, any cash we get go in the pocket, not in your nose or fucked-up arm."

After, when he had lain on a sweat-soaked bed for an additional week, trying to decide if he should kill his brother or kill himself, he became aware of the texture of his own skin once more. Breathed in the scent of rain. Bathed. Ate and actually tasted what was on his tongue. He was able somehow to focus beyond the next hit and his rage slowly dissipated. He had been on the other side of hell and now that he was back, it seemed so simple. Tito had still ragged him for being thin and jumpy but at least it wasn't that monkey making him jump. Tito had saved his life. And now he was gone.

In the dim light, he watched his mother watch him. "So where was you?" she whispered.

"Ma, I—I hadda lay kinda low . . ."

"What happened?"

As she spoke, she moved again to settle into a ruined overstuffed chair and folded her arms across her collapsed chest. Her face now appeared seamed, like old stitched leather, and her eyes were clouded from cataracts. Her breathing was heavy, and he could think of nothing to say except "Whyn't you git ridda them stupid cats. They makin' your asthma act up."

She leaned forward and her eyes widened.

"You don't worry about my asthma. You worry about your sorry behind. Junior's body smash so bad, I hardly recognized 'im except for that mark on his shoulder."

"How you find out?"

"Pee-Wee was in Thelma's and heard somethin' down the bar. Said somebody had either got dumped or jumped from the viaduct. Somebody in the crowd saw the mark and told him. He come by here, askin' about him. That's how I know. You don't see too many tattoos shaped like a swan. Said they was even jokin' about it uptown, that somebody took a swan dive. Pee kinda figured out who it was but don't believe Tito jumped. He wouldn't've done that. And papers say somebody got stabbed."

Conroy did not answer. Instead he rose to look out the window. It was past midnight. The gauze of pink and gray that earlier obscured the moon had drifted past, and the decrepit facades of the buildings across the street took on a ghostly sheen.

He gazed toward Lenox Avenue and was surprised to see a small knot of people strolling through the block, three men and two women, moving toward the glow of Seventh Avenue.

Two of the men wore light poplin suits with pale ties; the other wore a leather vest and chinos. The women, dressed in silk prints, strolled a step ahead of the men. Suddenly one screamed and jumped back. "You see that?"

"What?"

"Oh my God, it was the biggest rodent I ever saw."

They picked up their pace and the thin laughter drifted in their wake.

Conroy watched them until they were out of sight. Rodent. He repeated the word and felt something rise in him like wonder. They were probably from Sugar Hill, where the rats have different names. Finally he turned from the window to face his mother again.

"It was an accident," he whispered.

"Accident? They say somebody got stabbed."

He fidgeted, stared into the dark, avoiding her gaze. "Well, maybe . . . you know, stuff happen so fast. We had the setup, but it went wrong. It just went wrong."

"What?"

"Well, this guy owed us some dollars, a lotta dollars, and we tried to talk to him. Next thing we know, he jumped bad, ran all over Tito. Had 'im down on the ground, kickin' 'im. Bad stuff, you know. Then the guy all of sudden knocked 'im over the railin'. Just like that. For no reason, it happened just like that."

There was nothing in his mother's gaze that said she believed him. Her lower lip was drawn into the space where her teeth should have been, and her thin gray hair was parted in the center and drawn back in a small bun at the nape of her neck. He felt his eyes begin to water and he scrambled for something to say, anything to deflect her stare, but nothing came.

"And so you couldn't find your way to the funeral?"

"Look, Ma—"

"Uh, uh. You look. Your brother's gone and I'm left with a bill I don't know how I'm gonna pay. Funerals don't get done for free, you know. I had to go to Savoy. As much business as you gave him, that's the least he coulda done . . ."

Conroy had turned to the window again but wheeled around at the mention of the name.

"Savoy? Ma, you went to him?"

"What was I supposed to do? I told him you'd take care of it and he said okay."

Savoy was the Harlem Shark, and Conroy knew more than a few people confined to wheelchairs because they had been late with a payment.

"Listen, Ma. I'll take care of it."

He was talking fast even though he had nothing to hook on to. "I'm gonna look into somethin'—a little thing I was thinkin' of gettin' into. Woulda been into it, both me and Tito, if that sucka hadda given up what he owed us. Now we, I mean—"

"So what you gonna do? Get a job, maybe? I been tellin' you all along it's easier to do nine to five for forty hours than it is to do twenty-four hours for twenty-four years but you don't want to listen."

"I'm listenin' and you right. I'm gonna see about that. I got some plans."

"You know Savoy ain't gonna wait but so long."

"I know that too."

He heard more laughter from the street and moved away from the window to stand in the dark center of the room. He was able to think better away from the sounds. The strollers below had plans, destinations, if only for the evening. They knew where they were going. His own mind was a blank and he hoped his mother would not press him further. This was one damn complication piled on another. Tito dead, Savoy counting the days, probably combin' the spots for him right now.

The candles had burned down and some had guttered out, leaving a brief heavy scent of burnt wax in the air. From the smaller room off the living room, he heard the cry of the two cats his mother had taken in and refused to get rid of.

"Rat insurance," she had called them.

More candles burned out and his mother's presence was lost in the dark. He listened to the ragged sound of her breathing. It was like a murmur just below the crying cats. He thought of his brother, who would have known what to do. But Tito was gone. He wasn't coming back like he had come back that time from Dannemora.

Conroy drew a deep breath. *That wasn't no way for you to go, Tito. No way. Gotta make it up to you. I gotta make it right.*

CHAPTER 6

*M*arin had to move slowly, and Margaret understood. Chancey understood also but his grip on Marin's arm was still tight when they stepped from his car. Marin and Margaret lived in the corner house off Eighth Avenue across the street from the Peacock bar, and the stoop was crowded with loungers, as if they had gathered to welcome him home. Mr. Hamilton, the grocer next door, waved. "Glad you back, brother. Take it easy. You be on your feet in no time."

Marin smiled. "Glad to be home."

Some in the crowd offered advice as they parted, allowing him to pass. "Damn good what you did, Marin. Somebody try to off me, I'd do the same thing."

He nodded and said nothing. Evidently, Detective Benjamin or his partner had made the rounds, notepad in hand and questions on their minds.

"Good to be home," he said again and lost his smile when he thought of Benjamin's partner.

Damn sommabitch talkin' that shit about drugs. Like every black man is into that . . .

The steps weren't so bad, although he had to take them one at a time and pause to rest in between. When they reached the landing and Margaret put the key in the door, he breathed in quickly and deeply, sucking in the air as if he had just emerged from underwater.

Chance did not enter but left them at the door. "Okay, my man. Catch you later. Call me if you need anything. Don't forget, call me."

They watched him take the stairs down two at a time.

In the apartment, Marin's gaze took in the familiar objects. Nothing had changed but he stared anyway, looked around, studying in detail the same way he stared when he had returned home with his army bag slung over his shoulder: Sun filtered through the blinds. The kitchen had the formica dinette set; the teapot was on the back burner of the old stove, and in the corner rested the small doily-covered fridge with the loud motor that let them know every time they opened it that it was still working hard.

The bedroom with its patterned wallpaper had space enough for the iron bed and two small night tables. The quilt that had belonged to Margaret's grandmother was folded at the bottom of the bed.

He liked the kitchen but spent most of the time in the living room because that's where the sun set in the evenings. On a clear day, its fading rays bathed the sofa, the easy chair, and the broken grandfather clock in pale magenta.

Marin eased into the chair. All he wanted to do was relax. He watched Margaret move around him, slow and heavy, and wasn't sure if it was the heat or the weight but he knew he had to get himself together. There was no time. She seemed ready to go into the hospital at any moment.

In the few minutes it had taken her to fix the tea and return to the living room, he had fallen asleep. She did not wake him but sat on the sofa facing him and closed her eyes. She was tired, her lower back seemed about to break, her ankles were swollen, and she felt a sudden irrational surge of anger toward the unborn child for rendering her in such an awkward, heavy, and helpless state.

Nine months had begun to feel like nine years since they had gone dancing at the Rennie Ballroom, tasted chicken and waffles at Wells' Restaurant at three in the morning, or stopped in on a late-night session at Minton's Playhouse.

The best time she remembered was sitting at the bar the night Thelonious Monk strolled in after his gig at the Five Spot. She watched him lean over the keys, close his eyes, and run his fingers down the chords. The other musicians struck up but Monk played as if he were alone in the place, listening to notes that only he seemed to hear. There were solos and duets and the crowd sat spellbound till dawn. It was hard getting to work the next morning, but it was the best night out she ever remembered.

She gazed at Marin, sound asleep, his chin on his chest and his slender fingers resting on the arms of the chair. One hand was swollen slightly, and she imagined that he had hit the mugger hard in the confrontation. Her eyes settled on her own swollen stomach and she realized that she was not angry at him but at herself. Marin did, always did, the best he could. The pregnancy happened because this was what she had wanted and she had not planned beyond it, had not imagined the weight gain and the awkwardness that came as part of the deal.

There was no television to keep her occupied while Marin had been working, and now since this awful thing on the viaduct, there probably wouldn't ever be one. Which was okay. Marin was alive. That was enough. Maybe tonight he could rub her stomach again with the light olive oil the way he used to. He loved doing that and it helped her withstand the hurtful observations of the neighbors every time she lumbered downstairs.

"Girl, you still here?"

"Must be twins . . . or a mighty big baby."

"Girl, you huge! You hear me? Huge! When you due?"

She had only lifted her shoulders and smiled, too tired to open her mouth wide enough to tell them to mind their own damn business. And now this thing was happening. How could so much hit them all at one time? If she had been in any shape, she could've at least gone back to her old keypunch job until times got better. But—

They both snapped awake at the sound. Her teacup had fallen from her hands and lay in pieces at her feet.

"Damn it! Damn it!"

Marin stared at her in surprise. He had never heard her use hard language as long as he had known her. "Baby, wait a minute. Relax. It's only a teacup."

Only a teacup. She could not bend down to clean it up. She couldn't bend.

Marin moved from the chair to sit beside her. The sudden effort caused something like an electric charge to cut through him and he held his breath, held tightly to the hope that it would pass and not return—at least for a while—until he could calm her down.

"It's only a cup. A saucer. Why you cryin', baby?"

"I don't know, I feel so—"

"Look. Soon as I'm on my feet again, I'll buy you a whole set. A whole new set, okay? Ain't nuthin' to cry about."

He held her head against his shoulder and felt the current of agitation as she wept.

"Everything's gonna be all right, Margaret. I promise. We hit a rough spot but this ain't but a bump in the road. I'll get some unemployment for a while, then I'll find something. We ain't endin' up on no welfare, either. I can promise you that. We got four hundred and eighty-three dollars in the bank. That'll hold us till the unemployment checks come. We gonna be fine. I love you, baby. I love you more than life."

He held her until the shaking subsided.

He had wanted to mention the earlier bad times, how she had stuck by him, held him, whispered in his ear in the middle of the night when he woke trembling from the nightmare that had followed him home from 'Nam, had lain like a seed, dormant, then blossomed to monstrous proportions in the dark, in dreams where he had the M-16 aimed, and someone else held a gun to the side of his neck, just under the bone near his ear, giving him an order he could not carry out.

In the 120-degree night, the steel muzzle was like ice against his neck. Something blurred his vision and he was not certain if it was sweat or tears pouring down his face. His fatigues stuck to his skin, chilling him, and he was overcome by the odor of his own fear.

Then the blast. Close and sudden, and when he woke, he was in the hospital staring up at the ragged tent.

What had happened? The medic never asked, but he himself wanted to know. The scream was what he remembered because it had followed him home.

CHAPTER 7

From his vantage point on the roof of Sadie's apartment building, Conroy was able to take in the wide panorama of Manhattan: the Empire State Building, the Chrysler Building's tower of aluminum hubcaps reflecting the sun, and farther south toward the tip of the island, the slender silhouettes of the Twin Towers, the new World Trade Center, rose in a haze of pale gray and white.

The trees along 110th Street defined the southern

perimeter of Harlem. Behind him, to the east, the steel webbing of the Willis Avenue Bridge stretched across the Harlem River to the Bronx.

Closer to home, he focused on the line of buildings to the northwest. Sugar Hill, the land of milk and money.

The crown molding atop the renaissance-style facade of 409 Edgecombe Avenue reflected the light like a diamond, and Conroy vaguely remembered hearing that Duke Ellington had once lived there.

He had no knowledge of the others—W. E. B. Du Bois, Thurgood Marshall, Walter White, or Roy Wilkins—who had at one time also lived there. The building had been so full of celebrities, it had come to be known as the "White House of Harlem." He did not know this, only that Sugar Hill represented money, power, and prestige, none of which he had, and only one of which, money, held a place in his imagination.

He looked closely at a Pan Am flight curving overhead, coming in low against the white sky on its final approach to LaGuardia. He shielded his eyes against the haze and saw the landing gears lowered. The sun flashed against the small windows, and he forgot about Sugar Hill and wondered where the faces behind the small windows had been. Las Vegas, maybe, where the real big money hung out. The plane disappeared in the distance before he shifted back against the pole holding a line of wash.

Las Vegas. The name danced in his head like a song. He wanted to skip out to a new life. Away from the memory of the viaduct, which seemed to be growing inside him like a tumor.

He wiped the sweat from his face and neck and glanced at his watch, an expensive Hamilton acquired a month ago from a drunk who had stumbled out from the noise and music of William's Tavern and had not gotten two yards when he was cornered at 149th Street. A cool, moonless 3 A.M.

In less than a minute, the man's pockets were inside out, the wallet in Tito's hands, and the watch gone from his wrist.

They had come out of the shadows slowly, worked fast, then slipped across Eighth Avenue and through the arched portico of the Dunbar Apartments complex. They ran, unaware that Bill "Bojangles" Robinson, Countee Cullen, Paul Robeson, and Matthew Henson had once claimed this place as home. They ran, and only the sound of their footsteps on the wet leaves followed them through the winding interior garden.

On Seventh Avenue, there were few cars and no pedestrians and they paused in mid-block under a dim streetlight to tally up. Three hundred dollars. A not bad payday. They dropped the wallet through the sewer grate as usual, split the take, and separated: Tito to his pad on Bradhurst and he, to Sadie's place on Lenox lugging a double order of Sherman's barbecue and a sixpack of Pabst Blue Ribbon.

Paydays was easy 'cause we had strategy, worked the game right. Hats, caps, stocking masks, and sometimes them reversible windbreakers.

The sun with its penetrating rays forced Conroy to move through the lines of wash. He settled in a shady corner, flipped open the box of Marlboros, and put a cigarette to his lips. It hung there unlit, clamped between his teeth like a small stick of new chalk. He checked the watch again, trying to figure out his next move.

Could keep doin' what we always did, 'cept now I'd be solo and have to check out the marks more careful. They can't be too young or too big. Maybe I could nail a few pocketbooks now and then.

He entertained the thought for less than a minute before shaking his head.

Too much static. Women screamed loud and some probably wanna fight, especially if they had a bad day. I remember Sadie, skinny as she is, get mad just before her period and throw stuff I didn't know she could even lift. And then there was that time a pot of boiling water barely missed my face by inches. I damn near tried to kill her . . .

Maybe, maybe he could a get a job.

The idea took his breath away, made him so uneasy he scrambled up from the slatted-wood box to walk the length of the roof. He meant to stroll until the thought evaporated.

The sun sent beads of perspiration down his face and he squinted at the skyline. In the distance, the Empire State Building rose like a needle in the shimmering haze.

Get a job.

A scatter of pigeons circled overhead and fell away, drifting on a downdraft toward the Harlem River.

. . . Damn. A job. Fuck that. I ain't cut a nine-to-five in my life and ain't about to break sweat for no chump change.

He lit the cigarette and retraced his steps, moving slowly between the lines of drying wash. A cotton dish towel, light and dry, snapped in the wind, suddenly hitting him in the face. He paused long enough to touch the cigarette to the cloth and watched a dime-size brown hole curl back from the flame. Then he resumed his stroll.

. . . I can unload this watch for a couple hundred. This ain't no cheap shit. Keep Savoy cool till I figure out somethin'. A plan of action, Tito called it. He was good at this stuff, not me. But I can't stay up here all day, every damn day waitin' for nighttime. Can't keep on dodgin' Savoy. Sooner or later, I got to get somethin' in my hand.

It had not rained for several days and a storm was overdue. Right now, the city moved slowly in a ninety-degree haze and the occasional breeze brought only more heat.

He leaned into the billowing sheets, daydreaming, when the idea occurred to him. He felt his heart beat against his rib cage. When he calmed, he drew on the cigarette so deeply the tip glowed in the sun, like a yellow diamond.

. . . 'Stead of goin' after that guy did Tito in, I was goin' after his woman. From that picture in his wallet, she looked kinda easy to hit. Figure I get her, even the score. That woulda teached him a lesson. Come to find out, she big and pregnant. Big and pregnant. What do you know? So now, I just wait. Git my ducks in a row. Not only git even with the motherfucka for Tito but I git me some real dollars in my pocket, no more fuckin' chump

change. Plus I git Savoy off my back, then I move around like the big boys, maybe git to see what Vegas got to offer.

He hummed aloud as he dropped the stub of the cigarette onto the sun-softened tar and pressed it in with the tip of his worn sneaker.

. . . Tito always said you can't go wrong if you plan it right.

CHAPTER 8

*M*argaret leaned up on one elbow and stared at the clock on the night table. One A.M. The ceiling fan had stopped and she wondered what else could go wrong. She reached up for the pull chain and the pain hit so hard she fell back on the pillow in confusion. Then she realized that she was wet; the back of her legs and her thighs were soaked and she was overcome with a sudden euphoric panic.

"Marin, wake up. Wake up! I think my water's

broke. I think—" The pain came again and she gasped for air. "Wake up. Help me. I don't want the baby born at home. We gotta get to the hospital!"

Marin was on his feet so fast he would have suprised himself had he had time to think about it. He slipped his pants on over his pajamas, and at the door, scooped up the small overnight bag. Once outside, he remembered he had his slippers on. Margaret sat on the top step of the landing, holding on to the railing as he ran back to get his shoes.

Another contraction did not come until they were downstairs. A cab stopped and the driver eyed her, wondering if he might have to play doctor if they got stuck in traffic. It had happened to him once before and he was not anxious for a repeat.

They had barely scrambled into the back seat when he put his foot to the pedal and his fist to the horn. Four blocks away, a patrol car cut them off and Margaret's drawn face was illuminated in the circle of their flashlight. They stepped back to the cruiser, pressed the siren, and were at Harlem Hospital in two minutes.

At 2 A.M. the emergency room was as jam-packed as the clinic at nine in the morning. Margaret was wheeled away, leaving Marin standing in the crowd to watch the swinging door through which she had disappeared.

He stared at the frosted glass and wondered what would happen if he decided to walk through and keep on walking until he caught up with her. What if she was having a harder time than she imagined and no one was there to hold her hand?

His own hand shook and his mouth went dry. He needed a cigarette but was afraid to step outside, afraid he'd be nowhere around if they called his name. He could ignore the No Smoking sign, pretend he didn't see it, step into the men's room and grab a quick draw in the stall. No one would know. But suppose they sent for him and he was not where he was supposed to be? Jesus. Suppose something happened and they needed him to sign something?

He felt the trembling in his legs but decided against sitting down. There was very little space to squeeze into anyway. Suppose he fell asleep and didn't hear when they called his name.

He spotted a small crevice near the water fountain and leaned into it, far enough so that if he fell asleep, he could at least remain standing.

Six hours later, he heard his name. A nurse in starched white stood near the frosted glass door, and the refracted light behind her made her dark face glow. She held her hand up and smiled when he approached. "Your wife and daughter are doing fine, Mr. Taylor."

The words floated in the air and he blinked, trying to catch them. "What . . . ?"

"A girl. You have a daughter. A baby daughter."

He stared at her, wanting to smile and cry all at once. He was a father. A life had come into being because of his love for Margaret. He put his hands to his face and stared blankly at the crowd. The nurse cupped her hand on his elbow. "Would you like to see her?"

"Who?"

"Your wife. I think she's awake. Then you can take a peek at the wee one."

"Oh. Oh, yeah. Fine, that's fine."

Three other women shared the room, and it was quiet in contrast to the low noise of the waiting area. Margaret's bed was near the window, and she lay with her eyes closed. She had fallen asleep, and he was afraid to wake her. Then she opened her eyes just as he leaned over to kiss her.

"Marin? Is everything okay? Is everything—"

He saw exhaustion etched in her smile. Her eyes seemed dull, and he wondered if they had given her too much medication.

"Yes, yes. Everything's fine. Fine. The baby's—"

"Have you seen her? She's so pretty—"

"Not yet. In a minute. I wanted to see how you were."

"Tired. Just tired, that's all."

"I know. I love you, baby. I truly love you."

She smiled, closed her eyes again, and drifted off.

Through the window, faint streaks of sunlight spilled through the gray, bathing her face. For the first time in a long time, Marin felt his face wet with tears. He leaned over again, wanting to say more but could think of nothing, so he sat for several minutes, listening to her light breathing, then eased away to find his daughter.

In the nursery, all the bassinets looked alike, except for the pink or blue trimming. The nurse moved through the rows, guiding him on the other side of the glass partition. At the end of the second row, he saw the tag on the bassinet that read Baby Girl Taylor. Inside was a small, pale, wrinkled doll wrapped in a light blanket and pink knitted cap. The doll squalled to life when the nurse picked her up, and Marin heard her before the door opened.

Once in his arms, she settled down, staring unfocused.

"She has drops in her eyes," the nurse whispered. "They're administered to prevent infection."

"Oh," was all he could whisper. He didn't know what to say or what questions to ask. He was awed by the bundle in his arms, the weight, the tiny nose, the small round mouth that produced so much sound. He felt slightly intoxicated, and fearing he would lose his grip, handed the infant back to the nurse.

"She weighed in at eight and a half pounds, is nineteen inches long, and has a small brown birthmark on the left side of her chest," the nurse added helpfully.

These statistics slipped past him. He was still trying to understand how all of this happened, the mystery and mechanics of the process. He watched as the nurse settled the baby into the bassinet, waved, and left him standing there, gazing through the partition.

Girl, you pretty. Just . . . like your mama.

His gaze swept the rows of bassinets—sleeping, crying, wriggling infants safe in this safe place.

The setting conjured up a different picture and caused him to turn away:

The two small children with old eyes clung to an elderly woman near the ditch. She held a crying, wriggling infant in her arms and she whispered in a language he did not understand, but he saw her outstretched palm and splayed fingers and knew she was pleading for their lives. Memory enveloped him like a spider's web and he could not push his way out.

He could not look again in the bassinet, afraid of what he might see, but turned and walked quickly down the corridor. He had to find his wife.

Margaret was awake, and her bed had been raised to a sitting position when he returned to the room. Her hair had come undone and was tangled around her shoulders but she was alert and smiled when he approached.

"You're right," he whispered. "The baby's beautiful."

He wanted to kiss her and talk and clear his head but the two women, sharing the room and walking in small circles near their beds, glanced at him every time they completed a round.

"Got to walk. Got to to keep any blood clots from forming," one said, meeting his gaze. "Had trouble with my last one. Don't want no complications again."

The other one nodded, and Marin wondered if Margaret should join them. The third, a small-boned teenager dressed in jeans and T-shirt, sat on the edge of her bed with her overnight bag on the floor at her feet. She flipped through the latest issue of *Jet* magazine with a vacant stare, oblivious of everyone.

Marin reached for Margaret's hand. "How long they keeping you?"

"I don't know. Probably the usual five days."

Her forehead tasted faintly of salt when he kissed her.

"I'll be back in a couple of hours, baby. Got to get a bite to eat. Okay?"

"No, tomorrow is all right. I'll probably be sleep again by the time you get back."

In the corridor, he took the stairs instead of waiting for the elevator and strode through the crowded lobby. He stepped out onto Lenox Avenue and walked fast, surprised when he realized that the pain in his back had not returned.

. . . Tomorrow, I'm bringing the biggest bunch of flowers in the world.

CHAPTER 9

Day 1

Shortly after the 7 A.M. feeding, a thin brown woman in a white rayon button-down dress and starched white cap entered the neonatal unit on the heels of a maintenance worker, who glanced perfunctorily at her name plate before moving out of sight around a small bend.

The area was busy with the low noise of newborns, and the woman scanned the room intently before leaning over the bassinet of Baby Girl Taylor. Then she worked quickly—checked the plastic wristband and lifted the infant out of the bassinet, whispering a lullaby-like tune. "Come on, baby. You goin' home with your mama. You're gonna see your . . ."

She walked down the corridor, and once in the stairwell, stripped off the white dress covering her nondescript brown jumper. She snatched glasses and a gray wig from the large, perforated canvas tote bag she had stashed minutes earlier, and gingerly laid the sleeping infant in the bag atop the white dress and cap.

"You gonna be just fine," she whispered, more to herself than to the child.

A half minute later, she was in the lobby moving with the flow of the crowd. No one looked at the gray-haired lady with the thick glasses hugging a canvas tote in her arms.

A car waited at the curb, the hum of its idling motor lost in the din of morning traffic. The man behind the wheel nodded but said nothing when she slid in beside him, hugging the tote. Her eyes were wide with excitement, and perspiration covered her thin upper lip. "I told you. I told I could do it," she whispered, hugging the tote to her breast.

At that moment, a head nurse making the rounds walked between the rows of pink and blue trimming, peered into the empty bassinet, and walked quickly to the mother's room. Mothers weren't supposed to remove the babies. The child had to be brought to them. Where was the aide? Had the child been taken to be examined? If so, why had she not been notified, according to protocol? There was no sign-out when she checked the log. The child was probably with the mother.

She fixed a smile of gentle reprimand on her face as she entered the mother's room. Two women were walking in circles and talking in whispers so as not to disturb Margaret Taylor, who was asleep in the bed near the window. Her baby was not there.

The small-boned teenager was also gone. The nurse nodded to the two women and backed out of the room, stone-faced. She rushed to her desk, checked the log again, and quickly dialed security.

An hour later, Margaret got out of bed and started walking. The other two women ate lunch and chatted.

"Going home today, but first things first. Have lunch, then pack. This my third child. I ain't rushing to get home to no diaper duty."

"I hear you. I'm out of here tomorrow myself. What about you, Mrs. Taylor?"

Margaret paused and smiled. "Probably two more days, I think. I don't know, but first thing I'm gonna do is go on a strict diet. Look at all this weight. I'm walkin' around with an extra person on my back. Gotta get rid of this in a hurry."

The second woman placed a cleanly eaten corncob on the side of her plate and leaned over with knife and fork, ready for the baked breast of chicken. She sliced into the wing and held it up.

"Honey, this only your first child. Don't worry about it. All the runnin' 'round you gonna be doin', that fat'll melt faster than butter in a oven. You watch."

The door opened and the head nurse, a doctor, and a man in a dark suit and pale blue shirt entered. The room fell silent and Margaret looked at the nurse's face, then at the face of the man in the suit. He was bald though not quite middle-aged and his forehead seemed to hold a permanent crease from too much worry or too many surprises.

He stepped forward and spoke in a low voice: "Mrs. Taylor, please have a seat."

"What? What happened?"

Margaret looked from one to the other, then at the two women. Neither of them spoke, but stared back open-mouthed. Margaret was too far away from the chair so she sat on the bed, holding the edge of the sheet in her fist.

In the hall beyond the door, she heard the noon noise of trays collected and voices calling. She heard a laugh, short and loud, at something someone said. The wheel of the medicine cart creaked along the waxed floor. Laundry and linen was dispensed. She listened to the sound of a mop strike against a pail of soapy water and wanted to be near the pail, to look into the unremarkable face of the unremarkable person wringing the mop. She wanted to smile and nod, and the smile would be returned and everything would be as it should be.

But she was here in this place and she felt the door of pain open in her heart even before she opened her mouth.

"What. Happened? What. Is. It?"

The nurse raised her hand to say something as Marin stepped into the room holding a large floral bouquet. He looked from one to the other. The room was too crowded. Margaret stared at him blankly, and the other two women seemed part of a frozen tableau.

The man in the dark suit cleared his throat and tried to speak softly. "Your baby is missing," he said. He flashed a badge and whispered again. "Your baby is missing."

CHAPTER 10

Sunlight poured through the wide windows of the conference room, highlighting the collection of African violets, New Guinea impatiens, and orchids crowding the sills. The room was large and the walls were lined on three sides with bookshelves that rose to the ceiling but Marin saw none of this. The ground had shifted beneath him, leaving him scrambling to put the pieces back in place.

Ten minutes earlier, Margaret had been screaming,

the two women were crying, and the nurse was attempting to hold Margaret's arm steady so that the doctor could give her an injection. In an instant, she fell back against the pillow, breathing through her mouth.

He had stood there as if anchored in a block of ice, wide-eyed, not believing, thinking that whatever was happening was happening to someone else, not his wife, not his baby, not him. He watched one of the women brush past, crying, stumbling over the flowers that had fallen from his hands. Then just as quickly she returned, bursting back into the room and adding more noise to the chaos that immobilized him.

"I knew it! I knew she'd do something like this. Took that baby wasn't hers and scrammed!"

The other woman took up the cry. "That's right. She took it. Tanya took it. Here we was all feelin' so sorry for her, too. I mean it's bad to carry a baby nine months and have it born dead. What she couldn't understand was that was God's way. Ain't had nuthin' to do with her. Instead of prayin', she act like it never happened. It did somethin' to her mind. I was watchin' her, you know. Starin' into space and not eatin' and all she was doin' was waitin'. Girl checked out and grabbed somebody else's baby like it's hers. That's the devil in her. When you catch her, she need to be strung up!"

The woman who had returned tried to edge past the nurse to approach Margaret, to hug her, but the doctor held out his hand.

"No. Don't disturb her. We're moving her to another room." The woman stepped back. Margaret's eyes were at half-mast and her mouth had gone slack.

Marin could not move.

Marin shifted in his seat and looked at everyone around the table: the head nurse, the head of security, the pediatrician, the psychiatrist, and the director. The director's secretary was already taking notes, but all appeared as shadows without substance, moving noiselessly across his field of vision. Talk spun around him like faint atmospheric disturbances:

"She'll take good care of the baby."

"Thinks it's hers. Won't harm it."

"What happens when we try to—"

"That has to be coordinated very carefully before we—"

"Can't afford any mistakes."

"Hold the patient here until we recover the—"

"May be better off at home. She—"

"This is the first time something like this has—"

"Must move on this quickly and of course quietly. No press. Don't want them to—"

Marin's chair scraped the floor. He backed away and moved unsteadily through the talk toward the door. His hand was on the door and he said, "What room is she in? I have to see her."

The sounds stopped. Someone coughed and he looked from one to another but no one spoke. He felt his hand curl on the doorknob, and a flash of heat rose along the nape of his neck.

"Does anyone know where my wife is or do I have to turn this damn place upside down to find her?"

Out of the corner of his eye, he caught the suggestion of a nod and the head nurse quickly rose from her seat.

"I'll take you to see her, Mr. Taylor. I know how upsetting this whole—"

He ignored her. In the elevator, he ignored the blinking numbers as the car ascended. He did not take note of the floors. It didn't matter. He was taking her home. Now. Today.

Margaret was released four hours later after Marin signed the papers stating she was leaving Against Medical Advice. Chance was waiting at the curb and stepped out of the car to help settle her in the back seat. They had brought her out in a wheelchair, and passersby looked but kept walking. Marin cradled her in the crook of his arm as Chance pulled away from the curb.

"Not too fast, man. Okay?"

"Yeah. I hear you. I can't believe this. When you called, I thought it was somebody playin' a joke, a bad joke, man. I mean, how did—"

Marin glanced at Margaret and cut him off. Her eyes were closed but he could not be sure what she might hear. "We can talk later. First things first."

The first thing he did, after putting her to bed, was call her mother and her sister. Both came in a matter of seconds, and more noise than he could stand filled his ears. He wanted to join them, meld the sounds, but he knew that once he started, he would not be able to control himself.

Chance pulled him out of the bedroom and out of the apartment to sit on the steps in the hallway. The crying inside came faintly through the steel door.

Chance lit two cigarettes and handed one to Marin. "What you think happened?"

Marin shook his head. "They say a girl named Tanya took the baby. Her own was dead when it was born and she—"

He drew on the cigarette and stared out of the hall window. Lines of wash crisscrossed the backyard, and he imagined a line of diapers among them.

"We gonna name her Meredith when we get her back," he said, staring at the lines. "That's what we gonna call her."

The sun had set but the lights had not yet come on in the hall. Marin's face was in shadow, and Chance could only make out the glow of the cigarette as Marin inhaled.

"Meredith," Chance said. "Yeah. That's a nice name."

Inside, a mother and a sister, between tears, were ministering to a sick woman, washing her face, braiding her hair, changing her linens, her nightclothes. Who, Chance wondered, would look after Marin if he should break? This was worse than anything that had happened in 'Nam.

"Listen, Marin. I know some folks. I'm gonna put this on the wire and see what come up. Girl in Harlem Hospital, must live around here somewhere. Can't just disappear. We gonna get your kid back."

"Suppose she took her out of town—"

"Naw. I don't think so. Got to have money to travel. From what you tell me, this was a spur-of-the-moment thing. Emotional and un-planned, you know?"

"So she gotta be somewhere around real close?"

"Bet my bottom dollar."

Marin closed his eyes and leaned against the steps. Chance was silent, wondering if he should disturb him, when suddenly Marin stood up. His shoulders were drawn in and he appeared stooped, older than his thirty years.

"You probably right, Chance. That girl's last name was, let's see, Hamilton. That's what one of the women in the room said."

"How old was she?"

"I don't know. About nineteen, maybe."

Chance rubbed his chin. "In other words, old enough to make the rounds."

"Yeah."

"Get your jacket. Tell your folks you goin' for a walk. No. Tell 'em you goin' to the store. They ain't gonna understand no walk right now. Not with all this happenin' to your wife."

Chance lit another cigarette and the flare of the match illuminated his brown face, thin and angular with sharp features and penetrating eyes. His hair was cut close at the sides and full at the top, a holdover from his army days, days they rarely spoke of.

His saving grace was his smile, that bright flash of light that dazzled when he opened his mouth. At five feet eight, he was shorter than Marin by four inches but more muscular. He liked to remind Marin that lifting bags in the post office tended to keep a man in shape.

On the street, the night had grown cooler. Marin wanted to try some of the bars but Chance waved his hand.

"Not yet. She about nineteen; we need to try some of the other hangouts, like the Sportsmen's Club."

"Near the old Roosevelt theater?"

"That's the one."

They walked past P.S. 90, a huge Gothic structure abandoned for so long that the trees pushing through the windows of the deserted classrooms were larger than the maples in the park.

No one was in the street. On Seventh Avenue, the door of Thelma's Lounge was open and laughter blended with the current of music and drifted out to trail them like a shadow. In the street, a file of cyclists hunched low over spiral handlebars maneuvered through evening traffic.

"Think anybody there yet? It ain't even nine."

"Well, we drop in and wait."

The Sportsmen's Club near 145th Street was a small dance hall carved from underground storage space a dozen steps below street level. Booths lined the walls, tables ringed the edge of the dance floor, and a long bar looped with miniature yellow lights took up the rear. Life-size cutouts of Sly Stone, Aretha Franklin, and Junior Walker covered the walls above the booths and changed weekly according to the Top Forty R&B on WWRL.

The bouncer weeded out the underagers at the door. Inside, the low red and blue lights made everyone look good. Weekends were standing room only.

Marin couldn't remember when he'd stopped going there, probably ten years ago when he'd met Margaret and both decided they were too old to mix with the crowd and try to dance to their kind of music.

He had met her on the subway just before Christmas on a day when a blast of arctic air had dropped the temperature low enough to set a record. He had rushed through the crowd up the slushy stairs at 125th Street to give her the scarf that had fallen from her shoulders. He still remembered the plaid coat, black hat, and her fancy black high-heel boots. Most of all, he remembered her mouth when she smiled. The red scarf matched her lipstick.

She had had four shopping bags, and hesitated when he offered to help carry them.

"You're right to be careful," he said. "You don't know me from a hole in the wall, but the moon ain't full and I don't bite, and plus, we can walk where everyone'll see you."

He had smiled a brilliant smile even though he was freezing in a light coat, and talked her into a detour at the Lenox Lounge for an hour of jazz. By the time they left, he had learned that she was a keypunch operator at an insurance company and on weekends liked rum and Coke with lots of ice. And she learned a lot about the printing business, where he operated an offset machine, and that after work he enjoyed jazz, Bombay gin and ginger, and an occasional Miller High Life.

The rain had turned to sleet and it hit his face like small stones. He accompanied her four blocks along Lenox Avenue to the stoop of a five-story walkup on 129th Street. She didn't have a phone but took his number and the bags and strolled into the foyer. He watched the high-heel boots disappear up the stairs before turning toward home, fifteen freezing blocks away.

The club had not changed much but he felt old and awkward stepping into the place and hoped he would not have to stay long. It was still early. The crowd had not arrived. Chance greeted a short squat man known as Door, who checked the IDs and knew everyone who passed through.

"Yeah, I know Tanya. Nice kid. Got in a little bind there a while back."

"What happened?"

"Got jammed and the dude walked. Left her holding the bag, so to speak."

"Heard from her lately?"

"Naw. But her sister, Eunice, she here every weekend. One of the early birds. Hang a minute. She probably pop in."

They ordered a beer at the bar, and before Marin could turn the cap, Chance nudged him. Door was guiding a slightly built young woman in their direction. She was dark and pretty with arched eyebrows and a thick Afro puffed above her round face. Marin thought of Angela Davis.

Chance gripped his arm. "Let me talk. You be cool. Everything be all right."

"Eunice, this is Chance and his friend. They was waitin' for you," Door said. Someone called him and he left the three of them alone at the bar.

Eunice smiled hesitantly and pressed her hand to her chest but up close Marin saw that, under the makeup, she looked tired. There were shadows under her eyes, as if she might have been crying.

"It's about Tanya, your sister," Chance said. "We—"

The slight smile disappeared and her eyes widened. "Are y'all cops? Wait. Let me tell you motherfuckers somethin' right now. My sister didn't steal nobody's baby. Y'all already come to the house, tore the place upside fuckin' down and didn't give a shit about the fact she lost her baby." Her voice rose above the jukebox and drowned the rhythm pumping from the sound system.

"She been through enough, you hear me? Enough! Damn no good man split, baby born dead shoulda been a blessin'. But no, she had wanted that kid; somethin' to hold on to, and it didn't happen. Come home empty and empty-handed.

"Then today, a whole squad of y'all walk through the door, scare her half to death, and left her wishin' she was already dead. What the fuck more you want? Leave her alone. She don't have nobody's baby!"

Her face was streaked with tears when she turned away, leaving the two staring after her. Behind them, the bartender had already signaled and Door came rushing.

"What? What's goin' on?"

"A misunderstanding," Chance whispered, pulling Marin's sleeve. "Didn't mean to cause her no disrespect. No upset. I—"

"Look," Door said, glancing from him to the booth near the wall where Eunice had taken a seat. She leaned over the table with her head in her hands and her eyes closed. Eunice was a regular and pulled her own large, free-spending crowd who would probably step in any minute.

On the other hand, when would he run into Chance and this other guy again?

Door dropped his voice. "Like I was sayin', I hate to do this 'cause you and me is tight. But I think you better vacate. You understand how it is."

Despite his smile, he had gone into bouncer mode, and his muscles seemed to flex involuntarily beneath his pinstripe shirt.

Chance nodded. "Yeah. We understand. We know. Sorry about everything. Look, explain to her that we only wanted to—"

"We only wanted to ask her a question," Marin cut in, "but she gave us the answer. Sorry to upset her. We didn't mean to—"

Marin could barely control himself. His head was spinning and he wanted to run out of there, away from the music, the girl, and the truth of what she had just said. The girl had not taken his daughter. Where was she? Who had gone into the hospital to steal his child?

Chance was still talking to Door. "You got any champagne in the house?"

"I got some Moët splits. Why?"

"Send some to her table." He placed a ten in Door's hand and hurried to the street after Marin.

It was a few minutes before they spoke.

"Where are we now?" Marin asked. He wanted to answer his own question and say back to square one but he couldn't phrase it properly. His mind wouldn't allow it. When Eunice had spoken, everything in him had evaporated. The police had wasted no time going after her sister and had come up with nothing. Nothing. Her sister did not have the baby. He felt his head begin to ache. When he opened his mouth, panic coated his words.

"Where is she, Chance? Where's my daughter?"

He retraced his steps across 145th Street. Two crosstown buses trundled past, heading in a barrage of noise toward the bridge to the Bronx. He stared after them.

Maybe she's on one a those buses. Moving away from me.

The buses disappeared in the distance, and he tried to focus on the stream of passersby, staring at the faces.

Across the street, music drifted from the Lagos Bar and he heard Marvin Gaye: "What's Goin' On."

The rhythm sailed into his head but took on a different beat. *What's Goin' On?*

Everything was goin' on! He heard a voice and glanced at Chance walking beside him, staring at him with a mix of fear and empathy. So was everyone else. Someone was shouting and people were staring.

At what?

He shut them out and concentrated on the other voice, not smooth, not soft, not Marvin's, that would not go away.

What's goin' on? What's goin' on? What's goin' on? And Chance whispering, "Don't break, man. Don't break now."

CHAPTER 11

Day 3

"*J*ust act normal and you be okay," Conroy whispered. Sadie lowered her eyes and held the blanket-wrapped bundle closer to her chest. Penn Station was so crowded, so noisy, the policeman gave them the barest glance before moving through the waiting area.

A second later, Sadie froze. Someone had tapped her shoulder and she sat incapacitated, wide-eyed, wondering what to do. She felt the tap again and turned slowly to gaze at a smiling middle-aged woman seated in the row behind her. She was plump with rounded shoulders, and her face reminded Sadie of a chocolate moon. The woman leaned forward, smiling.

"I been watchin' you," she said. Below the hum of noise, her voice was clear. "I figure that's your first baby, right?"

Sadie glanced at Conroy, stared at the chocolate moon, then started to stammer when the woman cut her off. "I know, honey. I can always tell a new mama. Bundle a baby up like he gonna freeze in ninety-degree weather. You gotta unwrap him. Let 'im breathe some air. Get too hot, he be in a world of trouble. You know what I mean?"

Sadie nodded but Conroy did not turn around. Instead he had quietly dropped his arm from the back of her chair and leaned a few inches away.

. . . Just in case. Hell, anything could happen. It ain't been in the Amsterdam, *but who knows? Deal go down, at least I'd be in the street and able to get her bail or somethin'. No use in both of us coolin' in the slammer ain't able to do shit.*

He opened the *New York Times* and pretended deep interest in the news of the day but listened as the woman spoke.

"I got three kids and eight grandchildren so I know what I'm talkin' about. They all down in Virginia now and that's where I'm headin'. Took a week off from the job . . ."

The pause left a void that Sadie did not know how to fill. She had always depended on Conroy to think for both of them so she remained quiet as the woman continued. "Ain't seen the little ones in about a year. Time for a visit. Where you headin'?"

"Florida."

"No kiddin'. I got relatives there too. My son-in-law, he's divorced from my oldest daughter but he don't miss a payment for those kids so we still friends. What part you goin' to?"

"Miami."

"Mmm, where the rich folks is. Lemme—"

The sound system crackled, announcing the departure of train number 64 with Florida its final destination. Voices rose, luggage scraped the floor, families kissed, and some cried. A mass of people moved toward the gate as the announcer droned on, calling out the stops in between.

"That's my train," Sadie said quickly, easing from her seat. Conroy had already picked up the suitcase and was moving with the crowd.

"Damn nosy bitch," was all he said when Sadie caught up with him. A line had formed at the gate and they slowed down. He put his hand to his mouth and dropped his voice below the general murmur.

"Now, you got your tickets?"

She nodded.

"And you gonna call when you get there. Let the phone ring once and hang up and I'll know everything is all right. Don't make another move till I call you, you hear?"

They had gone over all of this earlier but Sadie shook her head anyway. She wished she were indeed going to Miami—with Conroy instead of the baby who, when they had first gotten her, wouldn't stop crying no matter what she fed her. Formula, plain milk, hot, warm, cold. Finally she boiled water with lots of evaporated milk and a pinch of sugar and that did the trick. The baby calmed down and so did she.

She was glad to be leaving, even if she wasn't going to Miami. Atlanta was just as nice. Good to get away. See her cousin. Dodge all those looks she was beginning to get from the neighbors, or imagined she was getting. No one actually said anything when they saw her. Which wasn't often. But maybe they heard the child crying for the last couple of nights.

She rarely left the apartment and then only to get diapers and food. She had to leave the baby in the house, in the little pulled-out dresser drawer, which she had decorated with an embroidered pillow and a small pink sheet.

In the evening, she had taken the child up to the roof and cradled her in her lap while she watched the sun drop behind the ridge of Sugar Hill. The sihouettes in the red-rimmed afterglow fired her imagination and she thought about what it would be like to live in one of those apartments. One on the top floor with large windows and views of the Hudson where she could watch the sailboats drift under the George Washington Bridge.

When the baby stirred, she lifted her up, rested her against her shoulder, and expanded her dream.

. . . Couldn't take a chance going to the park. But in Atlanta, there'd be no questions or funny looks. This baby's mine and that's that. Keep low till Conroy say it's time to come back. Maybe in two, three weeks. Then he straighten out the situation with everybody and we'll be on our way. Hit it big in Vegas and when we come back, maybe we be able to move into one of those nice apartments.

She smiled at the realization that Conroy was so smart. He had figured that the baby's father was rich. Had just hit the number for thousands of dollars and had been bragging about it in the Peacock, Conroy said. Imagine that. Set up the bar and even bought him a few drinks. Imagine buying somebody a drink and never saying a word about the money Conroy had loaned him sometime back. She shook her head at the nerve.

. . . Some folks get their hands on a few dollars and their memory just seem to fade away. But Conroy got this ace. Always knew he was a quick thinker. Fast on his feet. Fast in bed too, but what the hell. I can deal with it as long as he got a way of drawin' those dollars to him. I can't seem to work at nuthin'. Too slow, the bosses always said, and I'd only last a week no matter what kinda job it was. But Conroy likes me anyhow. And he ain't like some of those others. Always had their hand stuck out practically at right angles for a loan. Usually about the time my little check come. Loans nobody ain't never paid back.

. . . Least with Conroy, he never axed. Now and then, mention some of the tight spots he was in so I didn't mind lettin' him hold a couple a dollars.

And no matter how late he stay out, he always come in with somethin' special. Beer, Sherman's barbecue. He know what I like. And he said I was smart, it's just that nobody ever gave me a chance. But he said he trust only me to help him get his money back.

. . . Sure felt good bein' in that uniform. I always wanted to be a nurse. Just like Miss Mary, who looked so nice goin' to work all starched and pretty-lookin'. Conroy said I coulda been a nurse and bought me a uniform to prove it. Said I looked kinda good. Like the real thing.

She could feel him next to her as the line moved, slowed, then stopped again. At the gate, a young man was arguing loudly with the ticket taker, then walked away as two policemen approached.

Conroy adjusted his straw hat, pulling the brim at an angle over his eye, then put his arm around her waist and whispered again, "Don't forget what I told you. No calls. I take care of some business, iron out a few details so everything be all right."

They were at the gate. She smiled but her eyes were bright with tears. He was so damn smart, it scared her just being near him. She kissed him hard, then stood on tiptoe to kiss him again just above the scar on his eyebrow.

CHAPTER 12

Day 4

"*I* know how you feel, Mama Pat. She's your daughter as well as my wife, but I just can't do what you're askin'."

He ran out of words and gazed at the woman sitting quietly at the kitchen table. The late afternoon sun streamed through the window, highlighting the bright cinnamon shading of her skin. Her hair, thick like Margaret's, was mixed with gray and coiled like braided rope around her drawn features. At fifty-three, she was beautiful, but since last week fault lines had appeared, deepening the dimples and producing slight indentations over the eyebrows. He saw fear and hopelessness in her large eyes, and her shoulders slanted forward as if the burden of her grandchild's disappearance rested there.

Margaret's younger sister, Naomi, sat next to her. She was twenty-two and a history major at NYU. She was as pretty as Margaret but her attraction lay in her softness, her ability to approach disorder with a calmness that earlier impressed Marin, but the days wore on and, to Marin, her hope seemed to fade. Now she sat across from him, struggling to hold back the tears.

His gaze wandered over the large kitchen, the formica table and metal chairs, the shelves of dishes and spices, and the rack of pots and pans. He studied the knickknacks Margaret had gathered and that, with everything else in the room, had defined something in their life. Now everything seemed worthless. The room felt empty.

Naomi had been quiet until now. Finally she said, "Marin, please. Margaret's in bad shape. She's barely eating. Won't eat at all unless you feed her. We're looking at a serious depression here. Do you want it to get any worse? I can't understand why you don't want to send her back to the hospital."

"Someone from the hospsital comes every day," he said.

"But it seems like they're only coming to monitor her. They have a lot to answer for. Probably have a team of lawyers working overtime on damage control. Meanwhile, she's not getting any better. If she were back in the hospital, they'd be able to—"

"No!"

They stared at him, cut by the vehemence in his voice. He sat with his back rigid and his fingers locked around the glass of iced tea, gazing back at them—one on the verge of tears, and the other whose face appeared newly old, dented by the shock of this unspeakable event.

He dropped his gaze and his tone was softer. "I know, I know how you feel, but if she goes back, I'm afraid . . . I'm afraid they'll—"

"Afraid they'll transfer her and she'll wind up in that hospital way out on the island where we can't get to see her? That's it, isn't it?," Naomi said.

"I guess so. Partly. You know the only time we were separated was when I was in the service. The only time. We were married three years and before that we went out for three years. You know that. We didn't make a move without each other. It's hard to explain but I can't let her go."

He lowered his voice. "We don't know where our baby is or if, God forbid, we'll ever see her again. I need Margaret here. I can't face bein' in this place alone, worryin' and wonderin' about the baby. Don't ask me to do that. I need to talk to Margaret, even if she don't answer . . ."

Naomi started to cry as she had done each day since Margaret had come home nearly a week earlier. She and Mama Pat had taken down the WELCOME HOME banner, dismantled the crib, and packed away the pink baby clothes.

Naomi had taken a leave from her classes, and now she and her mother took turns visiting each day to help feed the woman who sat on the edge of the double bed in the small room staring out of the window at nothing.

The first day, Margaret had refused to leave the bedroom and sat with her hands in her lap with her fingers entwined but she had been able to speak. A day later, she responded in occasional monotones. Now, there was only silence. As though she had fallen asleep with her eyes open.

Mama Pat reached across the table for Marin's hand. "I know you want to do the right thing, son. And we ain't here to question your judgment. This is hard on all of us and we got to stick together. The baby's gonna be found, I can feel it. You're a good man and a strong man. God knows you always did right by Margaret. I never seen love like what you two feel for each other. So I know everything's gonna be all right. We just gotta have faith."

She rose from the table and walked to the bedroom to say good night to Margaret. There was no reply, and Marin listened as she continued to speak to the silence. "We be back tomorrow, okay? Gonna bring you some of that oxtail soup you always askin' me for and I . . . ain't never had much time to fix. I love you, baby."

In that silence, Marin knew she had leaned over and kissed Margaret on the forehead.

She returned to the kitchen, and he walked with them to the door and leaned on the banister as they went down the stairs. Their square heels clattered on the marble steps, and he heard the door to the street open and close behind them.

The quiet closed in again. He peered out the hall window at the coming night and watched shadows paint the courtyard deep blue. From somewhere came the low and slow sound of Aretha Franklin.

He turned from the window and nearly stepped on the small white square lying near his open door. The piece of paper was folded in quarters. He picked it up and opened it, and when he read the single line, he sat down hard on the steps, fighting to catch his breath.

CHAPTER 13

Day 5

"*W*hat goes around . . ."

Detective Benjamin's frame overflowed the metal chair and he rested his elbows on the kitchen table to study the note. It was not yet 11 A.M. and the temperature was already in the low eighties. The small overhead fan stirred the heat from one corner of the kitchen to the other but he seemed unaware of the perspiration streaming down his face. He leaned toward Marin and kept his voice low, aware that Margaret was in the bedroom.

"Sorry I wasn't in when you called last night. You didn't leave much of a message. Figured I'd come talk to you. Alone."

What goes around . . . He gazed at the short sentence and turned to face Marin. "Aside from the obvious, what else do you think this means?"

"I wish I knew," Marin whispered. "Maybe nothing. Or maybe it's somebody's idea of a joke. Maybe somebody in the house is probably jealous."

"Jealous?"

"Well, I don't know." Marin rose from the chair to get the pitcher of iced tea and refilled both glasses. As early as it was, someone had already cranked up their stereo and opened the window to entertain the neighborhood with the sound of the Supremes. Marin closed the kitchen window to shut out the noise.

"There's too many things goin' on in my head and none of 'em is making sense," Marin said, pulling the tray of ice cubes from the fridge.

"Like what?"

"Like for instance, take this place. There's not too many couples livin' here. I mean half the women don't have no husbands, their kids don't have fathers to come by and see about them. Some of the women have boyfriends who always ready but ain't too steady.

"Who knows? A lot of these same so-called neighbors used to tease Margaret when she was pregnant, remindin' her every chance they got about how much weight she had gained. Got so she didn't want to go downstairs some days. Other times, she tried to look through 'em like they wasn't even there.

"On the weekends, especially on paydays when I was workin', I'd bring flowers for her and the stoop watchers'd make some remark, tryin' to act nice but I could hear the nastiness underneath. So maybe—ah hell, it's probably just some crazy stuff runnin' through my head."

He placed the bowl of ice on the table and sat down, staring as if the answer lay in the cubes if he could just pick the right one. "You know, I'm sittin' here and the more I talk about it, think about it, the stupider I feel. I mean, suppose that note don't mean a damn thing. Suppose it wasn't meant for us. After all, it wasn't like it was mailed in an envelope or somethin'. Or stuck in the door. It was on the floor. Somebody could've dropped it and anybody could've picked it up."

Benjamin turned his attention away from Marin, away from the fear that seemed to shut out the light in his eyes. He focused on the paper in his hands, studying it as if he might have missed some small thing. He held it gingerly at the edges, folded and refolded it at different angles, then returned it to its original configuration.

"How do you know this wasn't stuck in the door and fell to the ground when her folks opened it to leave? From what you tell me, the hall was pretty dark."

Marin shrugged, wondering about this.

"The thing is," Benjamin continued, "we can't afford to discount anything. You mind if I take this with me?"

"Not at all."

Benjamin slipped the note in the plastic pocket of the small notepad that lay open on the table. Then he shifted in his seat and pulled out a large handkerchief to mop his brow, finally acknowledging the heat that weighed in on them. His linen jacket, draped over the back of the chair, had wilted, and his collarless shirt, open at the throat, was wet.

His dark brown face was seamless, and Marin wondered about his age and the years he had been on the job and how had he managed to remain so rational while trying to figure out the irrational acts of presumably sane men.

"How many single parents in the building?" Benjamin asked. Then hazarded a guess. "About ten?"

"Yeah. There's five flights, four apartments to a floor. At least two on each floor with no husband."

Benjamin jotted a line in the small notepad.

"Super still in the building?"

"On the first floor. Apartment near the mailboxes. His name's Mr. Yancy."

"Okay. Like you say, maybe it's nothing, but it needs to be checked anyway. I find anything, I'll let you know. We got the FBI and two of our own on your baby's case. So far, the only person to see anyone near the maternity unit was a maintenance worker very early that morning.

"She said that a nurse—thin, medium brown, not too good-looking—had come in the door right behind her. Practically stepped on her heels. Wore a name tag but she can't remember the name or if it even had a name on it at all. We're still questioning her. She's an older woman with grandkids and blames herself for not being more careful."

Marin thought of Margaret sitting on the edge of the bed in the darkened room. He had been too upset to help her bathe last night, and before dawn spent almost two hours preparing her to face another day. She liked bubble baths but her hair was too thick to wash. He would ask Mama Pat to do that later. Right now, he was concentrating too much on a note that probably meant nothing. Nothing.

"It's been almost a week, and all you questioned was that teenager and a maintenance person? That's all you got?"

"Right now, yes. We have to move very carefully. We don't want to do anything to antagonize the person who did this. It might seem as if we're moving slow but believe me, we're not. We have the names of most of the visitors and workers who were in the building, on the floor, and in the lobby that day. We've questioned all of them at least twice and we'll do it again until someone's memory kicks in. All we need is—"

"Don't say all you need is time because time is something you and me and my wife don't have," Marin said. An edge slipped into his voice and he struggled to control it. "The longer our baby—"

Benjamin held up his hand. "I wasn't gonna say *time*, Mr. Taylor. And I understand how you feel. I was gonna say all we need is a break. A break. That's how things, for better or worse, come together. It's a confluence of ordinary things that effect extraordinary outcomes. If I implied that it's only a matter of luck and a break, I apologize. We're not sitting back relying on either one. We're working to make something happen."

He closed the notepad and picked up his jacket.

"This note may not be connected to your baby at all but to something else."

"Something like what?"

Benjamin sat down again, folded his arms on the table, and did not answer.

"Like what?" Marin asked again.

Benjamin raised his shoulders. "Like maybe a drug deal?"

Marin stared at him, not understanding. Then he said, "You know, your partner come up with something like that earlier. When I was laid up. What was that all about? I mean, where are you comin' from, man? Y'all lookin' at me like I done somethin' out of the way by defendin' myself. I was robbed. Stabbed. I don't know how the guy went over the side. That railin' is low. I walk down the viaduct all the time and wonder how it's ten stories high and the railin' was built so low. Anybody could dive off there if they feel like it."

"You mentioned the other guy. Said he might've been on drugs."

"So what? That was just a split-second observation. Where you goin' with that?"

Before Benjamin could answer, Marin was out of his seat and pacing the floor. "Lemme tell you somethin'. I am the damn victim, understand? Not what you'd like to call the perpetrator. If your partner is so damn convinced that every black man he come across is perpetratin'—buyin' drugs, sellin' drugs, doin' drugs—then fuck 'im. He can kiss my ass. My wife is a victim. She might never see her baby again. She's sittin' in the dark and can't speak and I bathe her every day 'cause she's not conscious of what's goin' on. Does that motherfucker care about that? What is this bullshit about some drug deal?"

He knew he was talking too much but couldn't scale back his anger to the point where he could think rationally.

He paused near the stove and stared at the row of cast-iron pots hanging on the rack. The largest pan had belonged to Margaret's grandmother. It was so heavy that Margaret at times needed both hands to lift it. He stood behind Benjamin watching him scribble more lines and a rage overwhelmed him, filled him so completely, the iron pan took on another dimension.

Just grab it. The big one. Bring it down on this motherfucka's skull so hard, he be dead before he hit the floor.

And everything'd be over. Over. I'd be free from every damn thing that ever happened. My kid is gone. My wife is . . . My job is . . . And the dreams, the dreams, they'll be gone . . .

"Sit down, Mr. Taylor."

"What?"

Benjamin had turned in his seat to face him. "You all right?"

"Yeah, I—"

"Then sit down a minute. Let me explain something to you."

Marin moved away from the stove and eased into the chair opposite him. He seemed unsteady on his feet, and Benjamin waited before he leaned forward again. His voice was even lower.

"We got a serious complication, Taylor, and it'd be better if all the cards were on the table."

Marin nodded but the fire had not gone out and he was shaking.

His vision had blurred, turned everything a bright spinning red, and he needed a minute to get straight. He leaned back, drew a breath, and waited for Benjamin to continue:

"Ran a check on the guy that went over the viaduct. Name's Tito Henderson, did a five bit for dealing; refused early release because he didn't, according to the report, want to be under parole supervision. Served the time, came out, and laid below the radar. Has a brother, Conroy Henderson, probably the one that stabbed you, but we don't know that yet. They both got yard-long sheets. One has a history of small-time drug dealing and the other, big-time drug use. Now, jail time don't necessarily take care of a bad debt, you understand? It might be why Tito took that dive."

"Where do I come in?"

Benjamin studied the lines on the notebook. "You were there, brother. You were on the scene."

Marin looked at the ceiling and listened to the dry whir of the fan. *And this motherfucka got the balls to call me brother. Ain't this some shit.*

"You right. I was on the scene. It was strictly coincidence and his bad luck."

"Maybe. Maybe not. Look. This is between you and me. For this kidnapping, the FBI hasn't exactly beaten a path to your door—know what I'm saying?"

Marin nodded and studied the Formica pattern in the table. In the silence, he knew exactly what Benjamin was saying and understood that, for the Feds, this was no big-time brand-name case for them. The other observation, unspoken but understood, was that Marin's missing child had the wrong skin color. If she had been a white baby, the FBI would be lifting hot rocks in hell searching for her.

"... So the FBI is only acting in an advisory capacity," Benjamin was saying, "meaning the locals, the NYPD, will be handling it."

"Which leads to this: Our headhunter wants to look good so he's blowing it up. A drug connection makes headlines, makes him look like he's four-star material. He needs numbers."

Marin stared out of the window, then pressed his hand against his chest. The beat felt like a triphammer.

"You mean they want to tag me to satisfy their numbers? I don't believe this."

"How long you been in Harlem, Taylor?"

"Born here. Raised here. Probably die here."

"Then you know the deal. You know all about the setups and the throw downs. Mistaken IDs that somehow never get corrected. I don't need to mention how many brothers are doin' hard time for stuff they didn't do. Especially drug deals. They know it, you know it, the DA knows it. It's happenin' as we speak."

"Well, looka here. I ain't gonna be—"

Benjamin rested his hands on the table. "I spoke to the bartender at the Fat Man and I tracked your former boss. He couldn't say enough good stuff about you. Said if you were jammed, he'd go your legal expense. Ain't too many bosses willing to do that."

Marin leaned back in his chair. His neck ached and he needed time to digest what he had just heard.

"Lemme get this straight. I need to get me a lawyer. Spend money I don't have for somethin' I didn't do? Hell no. All I'm interested in right now is gettin' my baby back and gettin' my wife well again. Everything else is bullshit."

"And I'm sayin' to you, Taylor, that shit—bullshit—is what it's all about, and as a black man, ain't a lot you or even I can do about it. I got twin boys, teenagers I lose sleep over every night. My wife and I chew our fingernails everytime they go out to a basketball game. It's like black kids are an endangered species and we parents got to worry whether or not they'll make it back to the cave."

He reached for the glass of iced tea but did not lift it to his mouth. "Didn't mean to go off like that but I'll tell you this also. My partner has his own agenda, and Dave Leahy ain't exactly a joy to work with. Like the few black cops in the precinct, I got to watch my own back.

So if Leahy shows up, ask to see the warrant. If he produces one, say nothing until you have an attorney present, though I doubt it'll come to that.

"Like I said, it's about quotas, statistics. It's about looking good for the big boys, and the head hunter doesn't give a damn how he gets the numbers. Now if what went down on the viaduct is your story, don't change one comma. I'll be in touch in a few days and hopefully have something for you." He glanced toward the half-closed bedroom door.

"Don't think about this note. Right now, you got too much on your plate."

He rose to leave and Marin was able to breathe easier. He had not meant to lose his temper nor prolong the visit but he was stunned by what he had just heard.

. . . FBI playing games. Black cops having to watch their own backs. Everybody worried about their kids. What chance do we have? What the hell else is goin' on? What does he mean by "stick to your story"? Hell, I told the truth. He ain't laid all his cards on the table. Somethin' else is happenin' and he knows more than he's tellin'. Knows I lifted the guy and dumped him, but it was him or me.

Like that other time. It was them or me . . .

The viaduct was a ten-story drop. The ditch by the side of that road had been only three feet deep and the hot night had been saturated with sorrow when they finished . . .

"Fuckin' drugs. Fucked-up cops. And fuckin' bullshit statistics." He rose from the chair and began to pace the floor. Things were spiraling out of control and he was caught in the middle. Again.

He thought of calling Chance but Mama Pat and Naomi were due to come through the door any minute. They'd hear every word and he'd have a problem explaining this latest development. Better wait. But maybe it wasn't a development at all, just a piece of paper that meant nothing.

He locked the door and went to the fridge to prepare Margaret's mid-morning snack, hoping that this time she'd eat without too much coaxing. Maybe if he fixed a lot of different things and placed the tray on her lap, she'd shake her head and decide on at least one. He opened the pantry, then pressed his face against the glass door and closed his eyes wondering how much longer he'd have to mix the medication with her juice.

As long as it takes, baby. As long as it takes. We gonna get our daughter back and we gonna get our life back . . .

The sound of the bell shook him. He checked the table, saw the extra glass, and hurried to place it in the sink. His jaw tightened at the thought of having to hide evidence of a recent visitor, but he knew Mama Pat. One question would lead to another and he didn't need that right now.

The bell rang again.

"Everything all right?" Mama Pat whispered. She seemed breathless and hurried past him with the bag of groceries.

"Yes. Yes. What's the matter?"

She went straight to the bedroom to look at Margaret, then returned to the kitchen to place the bag on the counter.

"I had a dream last night . . ."

She wore a wide-brim blue straw hat and when she removed it, Marin saw that her face was swollen and the shadows under her eyes were deep as bruises. He wondered how she could have dreamed anything when she had probably not gotten one hour's sleep since he last saw her. But he looked at the rack of cast-iron pots and remembered how he had stood behind the detective, and he realized that when things get really bad, some people dream bad dreams while they're awake.

"What's the matter, Mama?"

"I . . . it was about that young girl in the hospital. The one that lost her baby. I dreamt I saw that girl, saw her body, her shape and she was still pregnant, but the face wasn't hers. Didn't match. I woke up and sat up the rest of the night. I don't know. Sometimes I just get a feeling that something is . . ."

"No. No. So far everything's still . . ."

He thought of Benjamin and could not finish. He looked at the tray with all the dishes for Margaret to choose from and he could not move to take it into the bedroom.

"Let me do that, Marin." Mama Pat looked in his face and moved to his side, aware that she shouldn't have spoken her fear aloud. "You go on outside. Get some air. It's too hot in here and that fan ain't doin' nuthin'. Take a walk or something. Naomi'll be here in a few minutes and she'll help. Besides, I need the kitchen to myself. Got to fix this soup and you'll only be in the way. By the time you get back, everything'll be done."

He nodded but did not move.

"Well, go lay down on the couch. You look like somebody beat you over the head with more bad news." She lifted the tray and paused. "You sure you all right?"

He did not answer but walked to the bedroom. In the dim light, Margaret appeared as if she were cast in bronze. Earlier, he had dressed her in her favorite cotton print dress with the shoestring straps. Sunlight slanting through the half-closed blinds bathed her face in ribbons of yellow. He leaned over and held her to him. The bones in her shoulders felt as thin as a bird's. But her heart was still beating. He smoothed the top of her hair and ran his fingers over the tip of her nose, her brow, her mouth.

"I love you, baby. I love you. We gonna find a way outta this."

Then he took his key and made his way out the door.

CHAPTER 14

Day 5, Evening

*T*helma's Lounge on Seventh Avenue was dark and cozy and crowded with tone and attitude. Men in pale linen suits leaned against the curved bar drinking Chivas neat and listened to Ella and Nancy fill the cool air with flawless sound. They watched the summer-tanned women in backless dresses perched like queens on the backless stools. The women sipped frosted daiquiris and spoke of the comparative humidity of the Hamptons and the Vineyard and the effect on their sun-streaked hair.

One block away on Eighth Avenue, the bartender in the Peacock would have had to check an old dusty recipe book in order to mix a cocktail. Lucky for him, no one ever asked for one. But he could pour rounds of gut-buster "two-for-one" straight shots blindfolded, and any customer able to stand up like a prizefighter past the third round was recognized with a bonus buster plus a beer chaser. Thelma's was all right with the Esplanade set but for half the neighborhood, the Peacock was the place to catch the last digit, latest gossip, and loudest Little Richard.

Marin glanced at the bird's iridescent tail feathers flashing over the entrance.

. . . I step in there, they probably go "two-for-ones" all night long. They got the wire but I don't need no sympathy.

He crossed the street and walked past the bar. Eighth Avenue was crowded and people moved around him, rushing as if late for important appointments. A couple, old enough to be grandparents, strolled by pushing a carriage. He stared after them and wondered whose baby lay under the light blanket. He watched until they disappeared around a corner. If he had followed them, what would he have said? Or done?

. . . Nuthin'. Nuthin'. Keep movin'. Keep steppin'. Head on up to the Fat Man. Jimmy might of heard somethin'. Naw. Friday Night. Too many suits in the spot. Jimmy probably be too busy to talk . . .

Instead, he stepped into Mike Headley's at 147th Street. In contrast to the Peacock with its cavernous high-ceilinged space, and Thelma's with its elevated attitude, Mike Headley's was a small, softly darkened nook with oblong windows shuttered with wine velvet drapes.

Miniature blue lights ringed the antique mirror behind the oak bar, and Errol Garner's notes floated from the jukebox like chimes in a light wind. The quiet ambience attracted mostly couples but tonight the place was nearly empty.

He dialed Chance's number, then took a seat in one of the wide leather booths usually reserved for those who wanted to impress a date and/or needed to keep the rendezvous off the record.

"It's designed for lovers," Margaret had said when he'd first brought her there. Now he ordered a beer and sat alone.

He didn't have to wait long. Chance opened the door, looked around, then eased into the booth beside him. His black knit polo shirt and beige chinos were pressed, indicating that he was out for the evening and open to possibilities.

"What's up? What's this about somebody leavin' a note."

Marin nodded. "A piece of paper. It said 'What goes around.' "

"How you know it was for you? Was your name on it?"

"Didn't need no name. I know what it means."

In the dim blue lighting, Marin's face looked worn and Chance tried not to stare.

"Then tell me," Chance said.

"It means," Marin whispered, "that I'm gettin' what's due me. It means—"

Chance wanted to reach out and touch Marin's shoulder but instead he said, "Aw come on, man. You gotta leave that stuff where it's at. We back home now. What happened, happened. You ain't the only one got caught in a squeeze. Fuck 'em. Never shoulda sent us over to 'Nam in the first damn place. Fight people we ain't never heard of, git half our ass shot off, and come back home to have Jim Crow kick the other half. That's fucked up. We shoulda been blowin' 'em away right here, not over there."

"I know, but—"

"No ifs, ands, or effin' buts about it. You nearly got your brains scattered over that ditch . . ."

"Well, if it wasn't for—"

Chance raised his hand, silencing him and at the same time, signaling the bartender. "Hey. I'm changin' up. Gimme a double Black Label and water chaser. And give my man here somethin' stronger than what he workin' with."

Marin ordered a Bombay gin and ginger and they drank in silence. The sounds of the MJQ drifted from the jukebox. Three more records spiraled up the spindle, and Dinah Washington sang for six minutes before Chance spoke again.

"You brought back too much stuff. It's interferin' with your life. You ain't normally like this."

Chance was the son of a Jamaican woman who, thirty-six years earlier, had stepped off a BWIA flight at Idlewild fifteen minutes before her water broke. She had given birth to Chance in a corner of the waiting room while a circle of flight attendants held a blanket up for privacy and waited for an ambulance.

. . . *And had the nerve to name me Chance, she was so glad to be here. If I had been just a little faster, I woulda been a British subject, born on a British plane.*

Instead, he had been wrapped up and bundled into an ambulance where someone planted a small American flag in his tiny fist, making him, years later, eligible for search-and-destroy missions in lightless, mosquito-infested jungles.

He did not reply when Marin said, "Ain't none of us was thinkin' too straight when we got back, but I'm not lettin' nuthin' slow me. I just—"

"Slow? Brother, you are paralyzed. Any slower you be dead."

"Wait a minute! Just wait one fuckin' minute—"

Chance saw the flash in his friend's eyes and eased back, holding up his hand. "Okay. Okay. I didn't mean it the way it came out, but—"

"But what?"

"Well, nuthin', man. Nuthin' at all."

Chance put his glass to his mouth but did not drink. Better to say what was on his mind now, before they got too drunk to remember anything the next morning.

"What I mean is, your kid ain't been found. Your wife is still sick. You gotta make a move. Do somethin'. You can't wait for the man. Lookit the FBI. What they doin'? You said they ain't doin' shit because this ain't no big-time case.

"And baby got the wrong color skin so they throw it back to the locals to handle."

"Well, what they doin?"

"Not a damn thing that I can see. Fuckin' locals too busy tryin' to throw more shit in the mix . . ."

"Like what?"

"Somethin' about some drugs. There's two detectives lookin' at the viaduct mess from a whole different angle. Like the guy I threw over was shit-deep in the trade and I might've been connected to him some kinda way. The Man can come up with some powerful stuff 'cause they know they can get away with it."

Chance put his drink down. The MJQ had come on again but the sound faded and the small lights behind the bar blinked in a sequence that suddenly made him dizzy.

They do stuff because they know they can get away with it. He had been there, seen prisoners pushed from gunships at one thousand feet, heard their thin screams spiral into the wind, into nothing, not because they had not co-operated but because the men who laughed and made them walk into the air knew they could do it and get away with it.

He remembered his mother embracing him and saying, "Chancey boy, this is America, the land of the free. You can be and do anything!"

The men in the copters knew it. They were free to do anything and they did.

When Chance spoke again, his tone was dulled by a fearful feeling he thought he had left an ocean away. In 'Nam, he had been a reluctant witness to mindless arrogance, and now it was happening once more, right here.

"Now where in hell the cops come up with this drug shit?"

Marin glanced at him. "Numbers," he said, lifting his glass as if offering a toast.

"What?"

"The local head hunters need numbers. Quotas, improved statistics. They need to look good and a missing black baby just don't cut it. Don't make the headlines. If they get the right mix, they close this viaduct case on a manslaughter charge, with a dealer on ice, a man on hard time, and both of 'em black so nobody gonna kick. And the numbers look good. This ain't no big-time bust, but it adds up 'cause they do it all the time. And it's a two-for-one. Can't beat that with a stick."

Chance raised his glass to his mouth. His hand was clammy and the air-conditioning plastered his polo shirt damp against his skin and made him shiver.

CHAPTER 15

Day 6, Evening

*T*he threatened storm did not break but it scared enough folks to keep them indoors. Conroy sat on the steps of an abandoned building on Lenox Avenue, shadowed beneath the scaffolding, and watched heat lightning streak the sky. Sweat made his palms slippery and he knew he could not work like that. He fanned them over the concrete steps, and sandy bits of stone came away in his hands, drying them.

For the last three hours, he had watched the bar

across the avenue. Music blared, lights blinked, but the action was slow. He glimpsed only a few people inside, and even fewer were out strolling.

. . . Need some quick cash before I put the main plan in motion. Note got to be just right. Let the motherfucka sweat a few more days. When he hear from me, he be glad to pawn his mama to come up with the dollars. Right now, I . . .

He checked his watch and spoke aloud, as if Tito were lounging nearby, listening.

". . . Shit. Ain't nuthin' goin' on here. Too many folks partying in pairs. Only one loner so far. Maybe I move on over to Seventh. Check out Basie's Lounge or Jock's Place."

A sudden wind rose, and behind him a faded poster announcing some long-ago event rattled against the wall, scraping the beam like a pendulum. Conroy jumped, then settled back on the steps again to listen, straining in the silence to conjure a message. When none came, he glanced at his watch again.

. . . Shit, nearly 3 A.M. Take a walk.

He eased up from the steps just as the bar door swung open. A man emerged and Conroy sized him up, then waited to see if anyone had followed. He felt the hot familiar whirl of energy crowd his chest. The man was alone, middle-aged, thin, and slightly stooped. Conroy watched him stroll unsteadily toward Lenox Terrace, where the heavy money lived.

He moved a few steps behind, shadowing him, then quickened his pace and shortened the gap. They crossed the empty street against the light and Conroy sidled up and snaked an arm around the man's neck. Anyone watching would have perceived two old friends struggling home. But the man's breath had been locked off and Conroy extracted his wallet.

He ran, and his lungs filled but not with the familiar rush. Tito was not there to race alongside. He did not hear the heavy breath of his brother's laughter and the call of "Payday, payday." The element that had energized him in the past had evaporated and something else was snowballing inside.

He raced down Lenox Avenue and turned into 132nd Street, suddenly out of breath, but he had to keep moving. He sprinted past rows of darkened brownstones with gated stoops and curtained doors. Someone or something was following, closing in. Was it the old man? He had left him on the avenue sprawled on the pavement near Pan-Pan's.

But something, something shadowed him and he dared not look back.

In mid-block, a car, moving against the traffic pattern, slid to the curb so quietly Conroy thought it was floating. All the doors opened. Hands grabbed him, lifting him like a worn rug, and dumped him in the trunk. Before the lid slammed, shutting him in darkness, he caught the glint of a .45 reflected in the dim glow of the streetlight.

"If I didn't know better, I'd think you were avoiding me."

Savoy's voice drifted out of the dark and Conroy looked around, trying to figure out where he was. When he answered, his echo came back to meet him.

"Naw, Savoy, it ain't like that. You know me better than that."

He was tied to a chair in a dim cavern of some sort and Savoy, seated a few feet in front of him, lit a cigarette and waited. He was small, perhaps five feet six, and elegantly dressed, like a high-powered businessman visiting from another territory. But his skin had the texture of an amphibian. His eyes blinked slowly. His head moved, turned, smooth and fluid like an anaconda's. He sat with legs crossed, and his pale lightweight suit and white shirt contrasted with the dim surroundings. His mouth was like a straight line and when he spoke, it disappeared somewhere between his nose and his chin.

Savoy was perhaps fifty, and Conroy knew, if conditions were right, one on one, he could have beaten Savoy to death. He could have stomped him into the dirt without breaking a sweat.

To Conroy, Savoy was old, and he could not interpret much beyond what he saw so could not understand that the man facing him, notwithstanding his snakelike appearance, was an experienced bird of prey.

Savoy leaned back in the chair, watching. When he spoke, his voice was soft and pleasant, with a touch of Carolina accent.

"I'd think you were dodging me," he said again. He spoke patiently but floating beneath was the threat of violence.

Three men stood to the side of Savoy's chair and Conroy recognized all of them: One was a hit man for a drug dealer he'd done business with in the past; another was an ex-cop called Enforcer who had done time for raping a male prisoner. The third, short and stocky and nicknamed Fireplug, stood between the other two. All were wrapped in muscle and their hands looked as if they lifted cars each morning before breakfast.

Conroy felt dizzy. He could see that they were holding him in some sort of garage, large enough to store dozens of cars. His vision adjusted to the dark and he saw tires stacked against three walls. Toward the rear, he made out the dim shape of a compressor and an auto lift. The air smelled dry and thick as if the place had been closed for a long time.

He heard the three bodyguards breathing in the dark, waiting.

"Like I said, Savoy. I ran into a little bad luck. You know how it is . . ."

"No, I don't. Make me understand. Tell me why I haven't seen you or a dime of that two thousand dollars you owe."

Conroy's mouth went slack. "Two thousand? Two thousand? My old lady ain't mention that much. She said it was—"

"Whatever she said it was, that's what it was at that time. Few weeks ago. You heard of somethin' called interest?"

"Man, I—"

He felt the air move around him as one of the men stepped closer. It was Fireplug. His hand fell on Conroy's shoulder like a block of masonry. When he opened his mouth, his breath smelled like water left too long in a metal can.

"Somethin' wrong with your hearin', motherfucka? Dirty ears? Maybe you want me to clean 'em out?"

"No, I—"

"Answer the fuckin' question!"

"What are you going to do?" Savoy whispered.

"I'll get it." Conroy coughed and tried to keep the tremor out of his voice. "All of it. This week. Mattafact I was lookin' for you. To give you this watch. Worth at least eight hundred. It's a Hamilton. The real deal."

"I don't deal in timepieces, I deal in time. Time is money. So let's hear how I'm going to see it."

Savoy's face seemed to float in the dim light, and Conroy knew he had to talk fast, find something to hang his hat on.

"You know that baby?" he whispered, "The one got tooken from Harlem Hospital?"

"What about it?"

"I know where the baby is. Somebody's holdin' it for money . . ."

Savoy leaned forward. He did not blink and his eyes seemed to burn a hole in Conroy's skin.

"Kidnapping? Where do you fit in?"

"I know where the kid is, and when the payoff gonna be. It's real big money. Real big. You can pick it up and keep it all."

He heard a snicker behind him and turned to look into the face of the ex-cop, who had eased up behind him. He did not see the slight nod of Savoy's head, nor had he time to brace himself against the blow to his jaw.

"Motherfucka, watch who you play," Savoy whispered. His voice echoed in the darkness and came back to hit Conroy in the face. "Sounds like you tryin' to give me up on a federal rap and you home free, right?"

"No. No, I—"

"I don't walk into no setups I can't handle. You put my money in my hand by next Friday. Meanwhile I'm takin' what's in your little stash. When you run into the guy next time, thank him for savin' your ass. He was luggin' a heavy load. If it had been empty, you'd be lookin' at my face for the last time."

Conroy wanted to say something, wanted to know how much was in the wallet he'd worked so damn hard to get, but another blow to the head and one to the back of his neck and again to the side of his face sent stars flooding onto a brilliant red canvas.

CHAPTER 16

Day 7, 2 A.M.

*W*hen Conroy woke, he was lying in a dense patch of waist-high weeds behind the tennis courts near the Harlem River Houses. The roar of traffic on the Drive overhead made the ground around him tremble. The sudden blast of a horn jolted him and he was able to make out, just barely, the webbed structure of the 155th Street Bridge before the image, swimming in a field of crimson, wavered and disappeared.

When he woke again the sky was the color of river water and he thought he was drowning. The rain came in waves and beat like buckshot against his skin. He peered at his left hand through swollen lids and saw three fingers that looked like sausages bent at different angles. Only the thumb and forefinger seemed intact. His right hand had no feeling at all and it took fifteen minutes to roll over and rise to his knees.

He crawled through the darkness, then rose unsteadily to his feet to stagger out of the park and past Esplanade Gardens, where a security guard eyed him warily, watching until he shuffled across the avenue and out of sight. The guard then resumed his rounds, shaking his head at the notion of a drunken fool wandering aimlessly in the rain.

Two blocks away, Conroy collapsed again on the bottom step of a stoop and held his head in his hands. The rain washed over him in a torrent and he sat there, too fatigued to move. A door behind him squeaked and he jumped when a hand touched his shoulder.

"Well, if it isn't long-lost Conroy. Went out to the store two years ago and ain't been seen since. What're you doin' back around here?"

He could make out a vague outline of the woman. Her voice was familiar but the umbrella shaded her face.

"And what in the world is the matter with you? Look like you was dancin' in the fast lane with a Mack truck. Or maybe you tried to walk out on the wrong woman again. Which was it?"

Conroy could not move his tongue from the roof of his mouth. He nodded his head and hoped she understood. She lowered the umbrella and he could make out the slim form but her face was lost either in the mist of rain or in the cloud of his damaged eye. She leaned closer. "You want an ambulance?"

"Unh, unh! Nunh!"

"Well you don't look so good. You been drinkin'?"

"Nunh, unh!"

" 'Cause you know me well enough to know I got no sympathy for a drinkin' man."

Conroy could not answer. He could not think straight. A hammer drummed a steady rhythm in his head and all he wanted was relief. Instead he felt another shock as the woman grabbed him under the arms and hoisted him to his knees, then to his feet. He would have screamed if he could. Instead, he fainted.

He woke again lying on his side. The rug beneath him felt like a silky fur against his face, and dim images came back, cascading in slow, unpleasant fragments.

. . . *Shit, it's Thelma. How the hell I get back here? Where she find me?*

The scent of something burning pervaded the room, and he shriveled in panic before he figured out what it was.

. . . *Damn fuckin' incense. Still think she can dream stuff up, save the world, save me. How the hell I get back in this shit?*

He turned over and realized he was naked under a light blanket.

"You finally wake?" Her voice came from beyond his line of vision. "Your stuff's downstairs in the washing machine. Shoulda thrown 'em all away, dirty as they was. Blood and vomit all over everything. What happened to you?"

She spoke steadily but he heard only bits and pieces, then realized he was shivering but not from the cold. He did not answer but squeezed his good eye shut and saw the fist of the Enforcer, large as a football, curve to connect again and again with his face. And fear and memory returned.

. . . *Friday. What I'm gonna do? Can't stay here. Thelma can't keep her mouth shut. Never could. I'd be a dead man before midnight.*

Thelma moved into sight, adjusted the blanket, and hovered over him. She had not gained much weight since he last saw her, just a little thickness around the waist. Otherwise she was still straight as a stick, had the same round caramel face, same long straight legs, and that same short Afro that he couldn't stand and had used as an excuse to break up with her. Not only did she still have it but it was cut even closer and dyed bright red. Her earrings looked like small saucers and shone with an iridescence that hurt his eye.

She patted the top of his head as if he were a stray dog she had just rescued. "You lookin' better already. Be right back. Drugstore for more bandages, peroxide, and stuff. You ran through 'em all."

As soon as the door slammed, he lifted his head and scanned the room. With his limited vision, he made out a small sofa, leather chair, and floor lamp, though he could not see the shade. Too far up to stretch his neck without hurting. But from the shadow it cast, he knew the shade was probably draped in some of those glass beads she said was good for atmosphere. He blinked and panic seized him. Was the light dimming or was he losing sight in his remaining eye?

. . . *What the fuck. I'm as good as dead. Damn motherfuckas stole my watch and all my money. All them hard-earned dollars. I'm back past zero.*

He curled into the rug and watched the mosaic pattern on the ceiling blur in and out of focus. He was too exhausted to figure out his next move.

CHAPTER 17

Day 8, 4 P.M.

*J*immy was wiping down the counter when the door of the Fat Man swung open and Marin walked in. At four o'clock, it was too early for the numbers crowd. The bar was empty and Marin listened to his own footfalls as he strolled to his usual seat at the end of the counter.

Jimmy folded the cloth. He was brown and big-boned, but his thin hands expertly handled a martini shaker. He had recently shaven his head, and the scalp, polished to a high sheen, gleamed in the low lights as he leaned on the counter facing Marin.

"No need to ask how you doin', man. Hear anything yet?"

"Not a thing, Jimmy. Nothing."

"How's Margaret?"

"Not much better. Eating a little but still quiet."

"You need anything? Couple dollars to hold you until . . . ?"

"No, man. I just come back from the unemployment office. Place crowded like they givin' the stuff away but I be all right in a week or so."

The news of the kidnapping had finally leaked to the press and the *Amsterdam* had featured it on the front page. It was impossible not to talk about it. Jimmy poured a gin and ginger and pushed it toward Marin, who gazed at it but did not lift it to drink.

"You know, I've been thinkin' about somethin' my mother-in-law said. Somethin' about a dream she had. I've been trying to put the pieces together . . . and not make a wrong turn . . ."

Jimmy nodded but before he could answer, the door opened and two men walked in. The taller of the two waved and called out, "The last out yet?"

"Naw, Aqueduct runnin' late today," Jimmy said. "So far, only heard the lead and the middle."

"What is it?"

"One and a four."

"What?" The tall man snapped his fingers and headed for the jukebox. He turned in circles and seemed to bounce as he moved.

Now I lay me down to sleep.
Pray the Lord my soul to keep
Should I die
'fore I wake
Please slap a dollar
on One Forty Eight.

"To which I say . . . Amen." He pressed several numbers on the jukebox and returned to the counter, clapping his hands. "Even if I don't get the last, I got a fifty-cent piece ridin' the bolito. But keep your fingers crossed, boss. I could sure use the whole thing!"

He sang loudly, even though there were only the four of them in the place. He settled on the stool, slapped his friend on the back, and called for a setup. Jimmy walked to the center of the bar and Marin, wanting no part of the celebration, rose and reached in his pocket to pay for the gin and ginger.

Jimmy raised his hand. "Naw, man. That's on me. Anyway, where you headin'?"

"Not sure. I'll let you know when I find out. You hear anything, give me a holler."

Marin opened the door and Jimmy felt the gust of heat blow in.

"I'll do that, Marin. You take it easy. Hug Margaret for me." Through the window, Jimmy watched Marin pause at the corner. The light changed and a minute later he disappeared from view.

Jimmy understood how folks talk and how talk never stayed in one place. He knew but most of the time kept quiet and poured the drinks. At times, he glanced in the mirror over the pyramid of bottles and read faces imprinted with avarice, envy, loneliness, and lies; faces that disappeared behind the upturned glass and reemerged no fresher when the glass was slammed to the counter again.

He listened and knew all about the big-time bar owner down the way who had bought that top-of-the-line, top-down Cadillac for his favorite bartender when all the while his hardworking barmaid was thinking she had the inside track.

And how surprised she had been when she walked in on them after-hours. The bartender was on his knees giving thanks, his head bobbing faster than a woodpecker's.

And Jimmy knew the latest details about the minister with the deep voice that so rocked the sisters, but who also had deep pockets for little girls and even deeper ones for the little boys.

Jimmy kept quiet as the talk flowed. Sometimes it blew with the speed and surprise of a hurricane and almost knocked him flat. Sometimes it wafted in on a breeze so light he nearly missed it altogether. And then there were the rare times when the word was so bad it shocked him into silence and left him shaking his head.

A baby. Only the lowest of the low would do that. They said it was a woman. Either she desperately wanted it for herself or the child was now dead.

It had been over a week since it happened, and not a word, not even a rumor of a word had come his way. Jimmy knew Marin had other problems too, way before this happened, because Chance had mentioned bits and pieces of their days in 'Nam. Not much, but enough to let him know they had seen some tough times. How was Marin going to keep a lid on this new stuff?

Jimmy looked away from the window when he heard his name. The two men at the center of bar, already celebrating, wanted a refill. He murmured a small prayer, raised Marin's untouched drink to his lips, then forced a smile to his face. "Same all round?"

"Naw, man. My luck has changed. Lessee some top shelf!"

It was Friday afternoon and Marin knew that whatever he had in mind had to wait until evening. Time moved slowly and he thought of returning home to ask Mama Pat to tell him again in detail the dream she'd had. It had been a few nights ago but she'd remember it down to the smallest detail.

He thought better of it. Telling the story might make her cry. Instead, he walked down Amsterdam Avenue and detoured down the hill to St. Nicholas Park, where the high sound of children came to him. He paused near the playground to watch them glide down the sliding board, perform high splits to a double-Dutch rhythm. Some raced to get to the swings, dodge a ball, hang from the rim of a basket after a slam dunk. The sun had edged away and shadow filtered through the trees, painting the leaves glossy topaz. A light wind scattered a small mound of litter, and on a bench nearby, the sound of the O'Jays drifted from a portable radio.

Then the racheting noise of a chopper, flying treetop low, its blades churning the air into reeling currents. The landscape around Marin shifted, then disintegrated, and children the color of fine sand burst like a fusillade across his line of vision. He heard the cries beneath the static pok-pok *of the M-16s and saw them scatter and run. Their hair was aflame and burned clothing trailed smoking in their wake. Their skin had bubbled like bacon from the raging firefight, and the screams and choking odor brought him to his knees.*

He moved his hand from his eyes. The basketball game had come to a standstill; the jump rope lay on the ground like a gray snake. The sound of the O'Jays had flicked off and the playground was wrapped in stony silence.

Men who had been leaning over chessboards now stood near the children, watching. They saw Marin's eyes, wide and filled with something they did not understand and so fingered the blades in their pockets, prepared to right a wrong move.

Marin bit the inside of his mouth to keep from calling out and stumbled away. At 135th Street, he collapsed on a bench in a small triangle of park and breathed deeply but could not flush the smell of ashes from his lungs.

At 110th Street, the north end of Central Park, he knelt near the mirrored lake, staring until it lost its color in the evening haze. He remained still as stone as bits and pieces of memory fled across the water to melt like ghosts into the shadowy vegetation.

Minutes passed before his vision cleared and he was able to think about what he needed to do.

In the fast-moving evening crowd, he walked faster, outpacing everyone as he retraced his steps. At 125th Street, he passed beneath the Apollo's marquee where GLADYS KNIGHT AND THE PIPS blazed in circling lights against the night sky. Across the street, the light shining in the window of Busch Jewelers was equally bright. Without looking, he knew that the matched diamond-ring set was still in the window and still on sale. Seven genuine diamonds for $475.

He hurried on, wondering who had that kind of money to spend on rings, wishing he had ten times that much to spend in order find his baby. But all he had was a few dollars in Carver that were shrinking fast. Even the money from unemployment wouldn't amount to much.

He passed Snookie's Sugar Bowl on 138th Street, where the college crowd spilled onto the avenue. Then he found himself at 145th Street, waiting in front of the Sportsmen's Club. The place was closed but this was Friday night, too early for the party crowd, so he waited, knowing that someone would be along soon to open up. A half hour later, Door stepped from a taxi and stopped when he recognized him.

"You know, I was hopin' you'd stop by again," Door said, shaking his head. He manipulated a ring of keys, found the right ones, and turned several locks. Inside, he tapped a large wall panel and the place was bathed in soft light. The inactive disco ball refracted the radiance, and the dance floor appeared pockmarked with diamonds.

Marin could not remember the club looking this good, probably because when he and Margaret had stepped in that one time, the press of bodies had been so thick they couldn't move, and the volume of music so high it was useless to think about conversation. Most of the guys had simply walked up to a girl and pointed to the dance floor. Phone numbers were written, not spoken. He wondered if anything had changed.

"Step on in," Door said, glancing at him. "I think you come by to check on somethin', right?"

Marin nodded. "I need to talk to you about Eunice, Tanya's sister.

And to apologize for upsettin' her like that. Somethin' happened and I needed to know if it had anything to do with my daughter. She was stolen from the hospital the day after she was born. I gotta find her."

Door looked at him, then gestured toward one of the tables.

"Have a seat, man. I didn't know it was your kid that got snatched till I seen the *Daily Challenge*. I wouldna' acted so incorrect if I hadda known. When Eunice blew up, I didn't know what the hell had went down . . ."

Marin looked at Door in the quiet and wondered how much he really knew. "Some other stuff went down since then. Has she been here lately?"

Door rose from the table and his footsteps echoed across the hardwood floor. He returned with two bottles of Miller's, snapped the tops, and pushed a bottle toward Marin. The room was so quiet the noise of the small caps hitting the table sounded like firecrackers.

Door put the bottle to his mouth and didn't lower it until it was half empty.

"Yeah," he said, studying the bottle's label. Marin raised his own bottle to his mouth and waited, wondering if Door was trying to decide what and how much he should say.

Finally, he looked up, squinting at Marin as if seeing him for the first time. His brown skin had taken on a red cast in the subdued lighting and his eyes seemed to narrow as if he were looking at something he could not quite grasp. "She come back," he whispered, "but she wasn't the same. Drank way much more than she usually did. And talked a lot too."

"About what?"

"The baby."

Marin's chest leaped. "My baby?"

"No. No. I'm sorry, man. I meant to say her sister's kid. The one that died. Eunice kept talkin' about the raid, and all. And then she started mentioning something about gettin' even."

115

"Did she say how? Or what she was gonna do?"

"No. Only that Tanya, a few days after, had to be taken back to the hospital. Nervous breakdown, I think."

Marin left the club and walked down Seventh Avenue. The slight breeze smelled of rain. At 140th Street, the Better Crust Pie Shop was doing a brisk business, and across the avenue, Neferti, the new fashion boutique that catered to high-end sisters, was also crowded.

The Dawn Casino had not yet opened for the evening but the Rennie Bar had, and from the kitchen the aroma of fried chicken, red rice, and collard greens wafted along with the music out of the open windows.

Door did not have Eunice's exact address but his vague description was enough to lead Marin to the corner of 133rd Street. In the middle of the block, a small boy stopped bouncing a basketball long enough to point out a five-story building shaded by one of the few trees that remained on the block. He stood under the thicket of branches and pointed to the metal door.

"She live there."

The quarter tip brought more information. "Third floor, left of the stairs. Want me to show you?"

"Naw, I can make it."

The boy nodded but trailed after him anyway and stood on the stoop, bouncing the ball. His thin arms protruded from his Knicks T-shirt and his Afro was long enough to move on his shoulders each time he bounced the ball.

"You know, Tanya ain't there," he whispered. "They came and took her away. And man, did she put up a fight. You shoulda seen it."

Marin thought of his wife and a large knot formed in his chest, cutting off his breath.

"When did this happen?"

The boy passed his hand over his head, looked at the night sky, then at Marin. The ball went silent and he held it under his arms.

"I thought you said you was her friend."

"I am."

"So how come you ain't get the wire?"

"I heard something but not the whole story—"

"Well the whole block saw it. You know what? You look just like the po-lice!"

"If I was, I would've heard everything. And a whole lot sooner."

Another quarter seemed to placate the boy, and Marin entered the hallway. The noise of the ball resonated, then faded. He breathed in the thick mixed aromas of frying fish, and something sweet and tangy that reminded him of the meals Margaret once cooked. Muted sounds of television and conversation from behind closed doors followed him to the third floor.

He was surprised when Eunice opened the door without asking who had knocked, and more surprised that she recognized him. He had the feeling that she had actually been expecting him.

"What can I do for you?"

"I'm not talkin' in the hallway. Can I come in?"

Her gaze slid away and she sighed. "Be my guest."

She moved aside and he walked down a narrow hall that opened onto a large front room. He stopped under a bare overhead light and stared at a war zone. A small paisley-patterned sofa had been overturned and its pillows slashed, pale pink curtains dangled from bent window rods. A television and hi-fi console was smashed and the small doors hung on the hinges at an angle. Two chairs had their cushions shredded and a small table in a corner had shattered glass piled beneath it. Remnants of clothing were scattered everywhere.

"Well?" She had been standing behind him and moved to observe his dazed expression. "Want to know what happened?"

She did not wait for an answer but began talking, slow and deliberate. "You the one with the missing kid."

"And you're Tanya's sister."

"Yeah."

He watched her move through the debris to stand facing him. She was small and thin and held her hands close to her chest as if she had been caught in a sudden draft. Her pink tube top and white capri pants were clean and contrasted sharply with her surroundings, but in the bleak light she looked much older than when he'd first encountered her at the club. There was nowhere to sit and so he leaned against the wall.

"What happened?"

"A lot."

"I can see that, but who did this?"

Eunice reached into her pocket and pulled out a cigarette. The match flared and a second later she exhaled, blowing the smoke through the open window.

"My sister is all I got," she whispered, not answering him directly. Marin felt as if she were speaking to a presence visible only to her.

"She wasn't in her right mind ever since . . . ever since she came home from the hospital. And nobody to help her. It was like she was thrown away. The only attention she got was when they broke in here and wrecked the place lookin' for a kid that was not hers.

"You axin' me what happened? They was lookin' for your kid, which I tried to tell 'em she didn't have . . . They come in like gangbusters. How you like to have somebody pushin' you, pullin' shit out your closets and throwin' it on the floor, lookin' under the bed, emptyin' your garbage can, even lookin in the oven—like she hidin' a baby in there.

"Well, she was in bad enough shape but that sent her over the wall. All the eyes was on your child, your wife, your situation. Nobody gave a damn that she needed help. Instead, they came in and when it was all over, they walked out. No *sorrys*, no word, no nuthin'."

"And because of what happened, you had to get even . . ."

Eunice drew on the cigarette, parted the torn curtains to gaze out the window, and continued as if he had not spoken.

"We only a year apart, you know. She's older but I work every day and I try to look after her."

She turned from the window. Her face was bare of makeup, and Marin saw lines at the curve of her mouth that were deeper than they should have been. Lines that should not have been visible at all.

"They left my sister movin' like a shadow. When she had something to say, it wasn't to me but to the wall. I had to look after her but I hadda work too. I tried my best. One day I come home and the place is in ribbons. I mean messed up worse than when the cops tore it up before. Then she come at me with the scissors. Me. Her sister. I nine-elevened and the medics come, she fight them too . . ."

"And so you dropped a note. Got my address from the phone book. Or the grapevine. Harlem ain't that big, you know. Found out where I lived and dropped a note. As if what happened was my fault."

Her mouth tightened and her eyes shone with a diamond-hard brilliance.

"It was. Everything was all your fault. But about some note, you try and prove that."

They studied each other in the silence and her stare did not waver. Her arms were clamped across her chest in a vise and her feet were apart, planted like anchors into the floor, waiting. Marin felt a pressure snowball from somewhere inside him and forced himself to remain against the wall. It was hard. One wrong move and the girl gazing in his face, so fearless and so frightened, would be dead. She'd be through the window and he'd be calling Chance from jail.

. . . Just what Benjamin and his partner expected and, this time, it would be open and shut. One off the viaduct and now one from the window. His breath was coming through his mouth. He jammed his fists in his pockets and forced himself to remain against the wall.

"You know, the cops have that note. They match your handwriting, you goin' upstate. Who's gonna look out for your sister while you busy dodgin' them dykes?"

Eunice flicked the lighted cigarette out of the window, unconcerned with passersby strolling below. Then she turned to stare beyond him at the broken room.

"I don't worry about no lesbians. I can take care of myself. If I go inside, the first bitch steps up gets cut up. So fuck that stupid note. There's nuthin' nobody can do to me or my sister anymore. Saw her yesterday and they had her tied down. She didn't even know me. She's gone, so you do what you gotta do. I just don't care."

Outside, Marin leaned against the lamppost across the street and stared up at the open window. His hands were still shaking when he lit a cigarette. The boy with the basketball had disappeared and Marin wished he were still around—not to answer more questions but so that he could hear the sound of another human voice. All he heard now was the low wail of a young girl alone in a small world out of order and no one to make it right again.

The air had grown heavy and what stars there were had long ago folded behind fast-moving, gray-edged clouds. A mist crept in and minutes later, rain followed. It fell heavily, hitting the dusty leaves of the forlorn tree and the trash-filled square of earth at its base. He watched the branches bend in a wind strong enough to scatter the few passersby trying to make it home. His own shirt clung to him until it was wet enough to wring out.

He opened his mouth wide to taste the rain as he'd done a thousand times when he was a child, but now the water left a taste of metal on his tongue.

The downpour finally obscured the window and he moved out of the lamppost's dim yellow circle. On Seventh Avenue near 135th Street, he hurried past Mr. B's Lounge, where stragglers huddled for shelter under the canopy. A flash of lightning illuminated them in a landscape of ash white. Rolling thunder followed. Somewhere in the distance, a long hauler blew a mournful sound that reminded Marin of the warning blast of a tugboat. He kept walking. He would deal with Benjamin about the note. The detective was a reasonable man.

CHAPTER 18

Day 8, Evening

*E*arlier that evening, Conroy examined himself in the mirror and tried to smile but his face hurt when he talked so he kept his mouth shut and his running monologue inside his head.

. . . Maybe that aloe and all them other bad-smellin' lotions Thelma's into did some good after all. I can eat again, even if it's just baby food, but what the hell.

He gazed at the blue marks under his eyes and frowned. The swelling along the side of his jaw and under his chin reminded him of a bullfrog puffed and ready to break into a croaking medley.

He dabbed at the area with witch hazel and examined his face from another angle. It still looked the same so he turned away, wondering if he should smoke and risk listening to another installment of Thelma's sermons. He lit the cigarette, opened the small window that looked out onto the air shaft, and rested his elbows on the sill, allowing the smoke to drift upward.

. . . Fuck this. Time to put somethin' in motion. Pull my ass outta this before Savoy come scoutin' me.

Thelma called through the door. "Goin' out. Need anything?"

"Naw. Take your time. Gonna watch a little TV."

"Baby, you should try to get out, take a little walk, you know. Do you good."

"Yeah, I know. Maybe tomorrow I try that. Don't worry about me, baby. I'm good."

He waited until the door slammed and then eased out of the bathroom to see if she had indeed left the apartment. Then he put the chain in place in case she changed her mind and decided to backtrack.

In the bedroom, he plumped up the pillows, settled himself on the damask-covered bed, and picked up the phone.

"This is a collect call to Miss Sadie Brown in Atlanta, Georgia."

He gave the operator the number and lay back, staring at the swirl of mauve clouds that colored the ceiling. Thelma said the shade was restful and helped a person sleep. A soft voice accepted the call and he propped himself up on one elbow when the voice became clearer:

"Sadie's not here," the soft voice said. "She's gone."

"What?"

"She's back in New York. You didn't know?"

He felt the drumroll inside his head begin and the side of his face flare in pain.

"You didn't know?" The echo came to him and he wanted to go through the wire.

124

No, dammit. I didn't know. He wanted to say this but he couldn't find his voice. Finally, he opened his mouth and his words were so faint, he had to repeat himself. "The baby. What happened to the baby?"

"Why, nuthin' happened to the baby. She's fine. Prettiest little thing I ever saw. Sorry to see her go . . ."

"When . . . when did Sadie leave?"

"Lessee. Around two days ago. I took her to the station. She said she was goin' back home. To New York. You didn't know? Where you callin' from anyway? You—"

Conroy slammed the phone down. The mauve-colored ceiling spun in a circle, dizzying him. He had sprung up from the bed but now fell back against the pillows, breathing hard.

. . . What the fuck she tryin' to do. Mess up my action, get me killed? Maybe she about to cut a deal for herself and keep all the money. I'll fix her ass. Too damn dumb for a real job and think she can outsmart me.

He was sweating and the perspiration burned his eyes as he lay on the bed. He had to get out and track her down. He sat up again and eased his legs over the side of the bed. The bottle of aspirin was open on the night table, and he shook several pills into the palm of his hand and stuffed them in his mouth like candy.

. . . Been in this place too damn long. Feel like a fuckin' prisoner. Gotta make a move. Git that kid. Git my money.

He glanced at the clock, then at the pair of gray linen herringbone slacks and black silk shirt Thelma had bought for him. They hung on the door and the plastic package of new underwear lay on the chaise longue near the window.

She had thrown his old clothes away and this new outfit, she said, was what he was going to wear on their first night out when he was well enough. This would be a new beginning for them. They would forget all that had gone before and celebrate a new life together. She had whispered this one evening through a thick fog of burning incense as he lay on the floor next to her in the living room wishing he'd had some weed so he could better appreciate the occasion. But since none was available, he could only lie there in silence staring at the shirt and pants as though the pieces were sacred objects.

He looked at the clothing now and sucked his teeth. The aspirin residue was gritty and sour on his tongue.

. . . Shirt, pants, underwear. Still got my shoes. All I need is a cap and I'm good to go. Tomorrow when she at work. No. Can't do shit in daylight. Tonight, I'll wait till she sleep. 'Round midnight, then light-finger a few dollars, and ease on down the way.

He thought of dialing Sadie's number but decided against it. No point in warning her in advance. Just cut on over. Knock on the door.

. . . Tito said surprise is the best element. Better than a knife or a gun. Who the hell knows what happened to my key. Fuck it. Probably changed the lock. No answer, break the door down. Surprise the shit outta her.

It was still raining at midnight as Conroy moved like a cat along Seventh Avenue. He stayed near the buildings, and every now and then ducked into a doorway, not to escape the downpour but to scan the street. He narrowed his eyes, scrutinizing everything that moved. He watched the cars, their headlights blurred by the driving rain, pass in slow procession and disappear into the fog. If one slowed too much or appeared to stop, he pressed farther into his shadowy recess, shivering, until they moved on.

An old woman walked past pushing a wobbly shopping cart covered with plastic. She herself was draped in a thin plastic cleaner's bag, which did little to keep off the rain. She was so wet she no longer hurried. He held his breath and watched her look around, scanning the doorways as if trying to decide which stoop or basement might provide the best shelter.

Finally she moved on, fading into the mist. The creak of the cart came back to him in a whisper, and a second later, also faded. He crept down from the stoop and moved fast. It was only a few more blocks to Sadie's place.

The lights in the lobby seemed brighter than he remembered and it made him nervous. He glanced behind him and took the steps two at a time. On the fourth floor, he hesitated, then pressed his ear to the door and strained to hear the sound of a baby's cry. Instead, he heard footsteps, heavy and unfamiliar. When he pressed the bell, the door did not open and his voice echoed in the silence.

"Hey, Sadie. It's me."

"Who?"

"Come on. It's me. Conroy. Open up."

. . . First thing I'm gonna do is slap the shit outta her, teach her a lesson, teach her not to play me for—

The door slid open and Conroy looked into the face of a woman who was as tall as he was. Her frame filled the entrance. His mouth went dry and he made a show of stepping back to check the number on the door, wondering aloud if he had rung the wrong bell.

"I'm lookin' for Sadie. Sadie Brown?"

"She moved," the woman said. "And I'm here now."

She stared at him in the silence, waiting for him to respond. Her face was framed by auburn-tinted bangs that fell into her eyes, and the buttons of her housedress were undone at the top. Conroy tried not to gaze too hard at her bosom, which had a tattoo of a rose superimposed on a dagger dripping blood on the hill of her left breast.

He stared in spite of himself. Thelma's triple-pierced earlobes were bad enough; now here was a woman with a tattoo. The rose bloomed on a thin stem and he wondered if it would wilt when her breasts lost their plumpness.

"Uh . . . When . . . did Sadie leave?"

"Few days ago."

"Well, did she . . . did she say where she was goin'? I mean, I need to know 'cause she got somethin' of mine I need to retrieve."

The woman gazed at him in the bright light and he tried to smile, tried to appear friendly, but it wasn't working. The imprint of the rose and dagger had thrown him off.

. . . Why did I use that line? Why didn't I say I owed Sadie some dollars and wanted to pay it back? Shit like that always worked. Hungry folks hear money their mouth get wide, they take bait, ready to give up their mama. All for a little money.

He shifted from one foot to the other wondering when she'd finish sizing him up. He could not look at the tattoo again but saw that she had light brown eyes and smooth chestnut skin and guessed she might have been around forty, give or take a year or two.

She did not blink and did not smile when she answered, "I can't tell you what I don't know. I heard she left some things downstairs with the super. Clothes and stuff. Maybe you check with him."

He knew she was lying but before he could find the right words to let her know, the door closed in his face.

Outside on the stoop, he thought of Sadie and the baby and his plan for the money and a violent tremor shook him. He wanted to fight, rob, stab the next person who stepped into view but knew he didn't have the strength and this fueled his anger even more. On the sidewalk, he felt the wet seep through his clothing. His head ached and the side of his face felt as if he had had a tooth newly extracted. He put his hand to his head and tried to remember what Thelma told him.

Just close your eyes and breathe deep.

He breathed, and his chest hurt as much as his face.

. . . Check with the super. Lyin' bitch. House ain't had a super in years. Got to get this shit together. If I had the dollars, I could cop a splif. Tighten up my nerves like they should be.

He walked back to Seventh Avenue in the rain, ducked into the doorway of another building, and sat down on the high stoop. He lowered his head, trying to think of his next move.

. . . Her and that kid gotta be somewhere. That kid is my ticket. Now I got to go back to Thelma and listen to more of her shit till I figure what to do.

His head was still down when the tall slim man hurried past, rain-drenched, hands jammed in his pockets.

The slim man glanced absently at the figure huddled on the stoop. Maybe the person needed help. Maybe he didn't.

. . . Probably locked out. No key and waitin' for somebody to come down-stairs and open the door.

He shrugged and lifted his collar. He had enough on his mind. A wife sitting in a darkened room paralyzed by something she didn't understand. Baby gone without a trace. A young girl in a torn-up room crying for a lost sister.

Conroy looked up. The slim man strolled across Seventh Avenue, away from the bright lights of Smalls' Paradise. In the rolling fog, the lights winked like small sparks. Conroy watched him hurry toward Mr. B's Lounge, where people had crowded under the canopy to escape the rain. There was something in the way he moved, light and easy. Almost like a girl.

. . . Easy pickins if I'd had my blade; if Tito was here, and if I wasn't so—

Lightning flashed, painting the figures beneath the canopy a stark ash white. Conroy's eyes widened. The shock of recognition jolted him to his feet. His mouth was open and he smeared the rain away from his face with the crook of his arm.

In the seconds it took him to connect the man with the walk, the walk with the viaduct, the man, enveloped in a swirl of gray, moved beyond the huddle and faded into the fog like a ghost.

CHAPTER 19

Day 9

*C*onroy lay on the bed staring at the ceiling. His face still hurt and he didn't want any conversation, at least not this conversation. Thelma was getting on his last nerve and he wondered why he had bothered to come back. He remembered the old, rain-soaked woman with the shopping cart and decided this was better than nothing. He cut into Thelma's sermon. "Well, it ain't like I went that far, Thelma. I just stepped out for some cigarettes."

"In all that rain? You come creepin' in all soaked up and brought nuthin' back but a bad attitude. What's up with that? Where's the cigarettes? I thought you was tryin' to quit? I thought you—"

"Look, baby. I was gone three hours last night. Three hours. Now you lighten up. I came back and that's where I'm at. Right here, right now. I got no plans to go nowhere else, okay? Now, put it to rest."

"But cigarettes, I thought you was tryin' to quit."

"I am. I gotta make up my mind to do it gradual."

Thelma looked at him. Most of the day, he had been pacing the floor, wild-eyed, cursing under his breath about something that had happened last night.

. . . Gradual? He smokin' those damn Pall Mall Filter Kings and stinkin' up the place? This ain't about no damn cigarettes. And ain't about no nicotine fit, either. Something went down. Maybe he ran into the people who tried to take him off. Or maybe he called on his woman. Otherwise, why take a chance goin' out all by himself? Ain't no use makin' no excuse. I reached over last night and all I touched was a cold spot. That's not good. He's into something that don't have nuthin' to do with me, I can see that. And gettin' him to explain is like askin' a wall to say hello.

She reached for her keys and dropped them in her purse.

He was sprawled on the sofa watching TV but clicked it off when she walked to the door. "Now where the hell you goin'?"

"To the barbershop."

"Damn, ain't your hair already short enough?"

"Not to suit me."

"Well, what you plannin'? You comin' back here bald?"

"Now that's a thought."

"Thelma, if that's the way you wanna look, don't look for me to be here when you get back."

She dropped her hand from the doorknob and turned to face him. When she spoke, her voice was low and even.

"That's fine with me, baby. Just close the door tight when you leave."

"Say what?"

"You heard me. I don't stutter and you ain't deaf. Just make sure the slam lock is on."

"Now looka here, baby . . . "

"No, you look, Conroy. I can see this ain't workin'. Not for me. Not for you. I nursed you back from death's door. Now you want to vacate and spend your time runnin' around in the rain, that's all right with you but it ain't part of my program."

"Ain't this some shit!"

"That too. First time around, shame on you. Second time, it's shame on me. I ain't takin' no shit a second time."

CHAPTER 20

Day 10, Evening

*N*o matter how crowded and noisy the Fat Man got, talk had a way of sliding the length of the waxed surface of the bar as easily as the drinks. Each time the door opened, Jimmy looked up, hoping to see Marin. He hadn't been in for two days now and he thought about calling. Just to check. Even Chance hadn't seen him lately. As soon as he got a break, he was going to the phone and give him a holler. Meanwhile, he kept busy, kept quiet, smiled, and poured.

The two men at the end of the bar drank slow and spoke low. They weren't exactly regulars but whenever they stepped in, they kept to themselves, never set up the bar no matter how much cash they flashed, and never said anything, just nodded.

The bar stools on each side of them remained empty, perhaps because the others knew of their line of work and had constructed an invisible preserve, enclosing them in a ring of isolation.

They leaned on the counter drinking Remy on the rocks. The ex-cop was dressed in a three hundred dollar lightweight summer suit, and the Fireplug wore a red silk shirt and pleated sharkskin pants. The shirt was open at the throat to highlight his thick neck and the sleeves were rolled up to accentuate solid biceps. The Enforcer, they knew, had been blown off the job for raping a prisoner. And the Fireplug, just as notorious, was known to crush a head between his hands as easily as an egg.

Jimmy moved back and forth, managing half a nod and a small smile as he refilled their glasses. For a minute the jukebox went silent, and in the time it took for a customer to fish another quarter from his pocket and press more buttons, Jimmy caught some conversation.

"You got to understand. Savoy into so much shit, he ain't interested in this but that don't mean we ain't. I mean, what we pullin' in from his take? Not that damn much. Peanuts compared to—"

"True. True. Ain't got to tell him shit. We do the do on our own time . . ."

"Cop that bread for our own self. He ain't got to know nuthin' . . ."

"Sound good. Cat said the folks was rich. Ain't dealin' with the law 'cause they 'fraid the kid be wiped out. That means they'll pay. Might even muscle a little extra out of 'em."

"But how the hell we know he's straight up? Folks come out their mouth with grade-A bullshit when you got a foot on their neck."

"Well, all we gotta do is pick him up and find out. You know Paulie, the barber on 120th? I was in there today. Mentioned a red-head babe been cryin' into his towel about some man fit the profile.

Said he had been all busted up when she took him in and soon's the motherfucka git on his feet, he turned and kicked her in the ass. We find 'im, lean on 'im a minute and he be glad to give up what he got. Tell us where that kid is and we—"

The blare of the jukebox drowned the rest. Jimmy lingered, wiping the counter clean of water spots that were not there until someone called above the noise, "Say, Jimmy! You a part-timer or what? What's happenin' down this end? We ain't partyin' with no food stamps, you know."

Jimmy turned around, lifted a bottle of Dewars off the shelf, and headed toward the voice. "Yeah, sorry about that. More ice?"

As he poured, he glanced toward the other end. The man called Fireplug had leaned his elbows on the bar, pressing his hands in prayerful attitude. His hair was cut close to his scalp and his vanilla face was framed by long sideburns and a thick mustache. His eyes were narrow, and when he smiled, he showed teeth spaced like individual squares of Chiclets in his gums. The mirror reflected his grinning face when he leaned forward, and everyone heard the crackling sounds as he bent his knuckles one by one.

Minutes later, the two drained their glasses and dropped a twenty on the bar. "Keep the change," the Plug grunted.

They moved purposefully through the invisible ring and did not look back.

Through the window, Jimmy watched them climb into a late-model Caddy and squeal away from the curb as if they were being chased. They moved too fast for him to catch the plate number.

He picked up the twenty and rung up the tab, then stepped from behind the bar and lifted the wall phone.

. . . Maybe the talk was nothing. Maybe . . .

CHAPTER 21

Day 10, Evening

*T*en minutes later, Marin rushed in. He was out of
breath and made an effort to remain calm as he moved
to the end of the bar to take a seat—the same seat,
Jimmy noted, that the Enforcer had vacated minutes
earlier. The place was crowded and the volume of talk
had risen to overwhelm Gloria Lynne on the jukebox,
which someone had turned up a notch.

He ordered a gin and ginger and glanced around.
Folks were laughing, calling out above the noise, and

he wanted to close his eyes and remember when he and Margaret had done this, but he had to take it one day at a time.

"How's it goin, Marin? Ain't seen you lately."

"A little better, Jimmy. Margaret's talkin'. The medicine is beginnin' to work. She's startin' to eat more. Still can't get her to leave the room, though, except when she go to the bathroom. And she still cryin'. Sometimes she cry so hard, she fall asleep from it. But she's talkin' again."

"I'm glad to hear it," Jimmy said. He put a napkin under Marin's drink and glanced around, waiting for the chance to move beyond the polite talk.

Marin nodded and picked up his glass. He did not say that Margaret was beginning to ask questions. Where was her baby? The child was coming back so where had they taken the crib, the clothes, the tiny pink rattle, and all those blankets she had crocheted? And when he could not answer, she could not control the torrent of rage that poured out and over him. She screamed until exhaustion silenced her. And in the pause, they were both conscious of that silence that would have been filled with the sound of the baby.

Marin rested his elbow on the counter and pinched the bridge of his nose between his thumb and forefinger.

We only got to see our daughter for maybe ten minutes. Ten minutes. God, will we recognize her? Will we know her when she— Yes, oh, yes we will. That birthmark on her left chest. Nurse said so. Yes.

He lifted his glass and was about to ask for a refill when Chance walked in. "Got the wire. What's goin' on?"

"Jimmy thinks he might've heard somethin' but it ain't the right moment to talk."

Chance looked around at the dozen or so men and women in the place. Everyone was still talking about the murder of the local numbers banker, who had been ambushed when he went to make a payoff in the hallway next door to the bar.

Talk was that some cops were in on it. Or knew who did it. But everyone had to settle for the usual pronouncement that the "Investigation Was Ongoing." Even so, everyone had something to add.

"Shit, the body already shipped south and in the ground a week ago," someone at the other end of the bar said. "And they ain't come up with nuthin' yet?"

"Nope. And they ain't gonna."

"You know, Tommy Dee was known to carry couple thousand in his pocket like it was loose change."

"Maybe it wasn't enough for whoever stepped to 'im. My mama say the bad thing about havin' somethin' good is wantin' more of it."

"Hell, whatever he had woulda been enough for me. Wonder where it went?"

"You got to ask? Fool, where you think it went?"

"South."

In the silence, someone tipped a Moët split and sprinkled an offering on the hardwood floor, affirming Tommy Dee's departure, but they also acknowledged that his murder, like so many others, would remain just another entry in a ledger, soon forgotten in a bottom drawer of a metal desk in the precinct.

Chance eased onto the stool and rested his elbows on the bar. "Walker Black and water," he said.

Jimmy slid a glass from the overhead rack and spoke while he poured. "Maybe it ain't nuthin' . . ."

Against the background talk of the recent murder, Jimmy's voice was so low, Marin and Chance had to lean forward to hear him. His light brown face shone with a dampness that highlighted the sprinkling of freckles near the corner of his eyes.

"Here's what went down," he whispered. "Few minutes ago, two guys—you seen 'em around. The Enforcer and the Fireplug. Savoy's backup. Arms like greased beef, faces look like—anyway they was here, had a few sips, and was talkin' about lookin' for—"

He stopped talking when the door to the Fat Man swung open.

Everyone else also glanced up, then away again, to study their drink or the face of their companion. Marin followed Jimmy's gaze and recognized Detective Leahy, then turned back to the counter to cradle his glass in his hands. He saw that everyone else had also turned to the bar. All except Chance, who watched the cop stroll through the pool of silence.

Jimmy polished a glass and his knee pushed the button behind the counter, lowering the juke box sound to a murmur suitable for a wake.

Leahy glanced at the jukebox and smiled but Jimmy saw the shade of pink color his pale face. His hair was brushed back in thin strands and aviator sunglasses hung from his jacket pocket. His steps were soundless and he looked neither right nor left as he made his way to the men's room. A minute later, he emerged and walked to the door, ignoring the sound of the few glasses clicking in the silence.

Talk resumed, the jukebox came to life, and Jimmy spoke below the volume. No one mentioned the interruption, and Jimmy continued as if the door had never opened. "They talked about Savoy not bein' interested in somethin'," he said. "Didn't say exactly what but then they mentioned looking for somebody who might have knowledge about a kid somewhere—"

Marin sensed the muscles in his face contract, felt the knots, hard as small stones, form along his jawline. He knew of Savoy, big-time shark, not only into money but also dope and prostitutes. Anything that brought in a dollar, he was in the middle of it. Talk had it that he drove a custom-made armored Benz.

"Problem is," Jimmy whispered, "Savoy don't hang out locally, at least not as far as I know. Got that big Fifth Avenue mansion with a private bar and disco in the basement. Heard that's where he trains the young girls before he turns them out. Whole place guarded by a pack of Dobermans."

"So I scout his backup. They was in here means they hang local," Marin said, pulling out a cigarette.

"And no point goin' to the cops on this one either," Chance said. "I pick up enough on my rounds to know Savoy got a whole lot of 'em in his pocket."

Marin was off the stool and Chance saw the agitation beginning to spill over. He touched Marin's sleeve. "Look, lemme ask around some more, find out a few things," he whispered. "Like where else the backup hangin' out. Then you make a move that's gonna be correct. Okay?"

Marin nodded, then sat down again. He was sweating. This was the first real break. Even Benjamin, with his network of stoolies, hadn't gotten anything yet. And the FBI—the do-nothing Fat, Bland, and Ignorant boys—were out of it. By the time he saw his daughter again, she'd be old enough to find her own way home. He had to do something right now.

He turned to Jimmy again. "I know of the backup but up close what do they look like?"

Jimmy went over the descriptions: the bulk, the weight, the flashy clothing that stretched at the seams when they moved a muscle, the canine teeth, and the eyes that had seen things ordinary people would not want to dream about.

"The Enforcer is an ex," Jimmy added. "Kicked out for raping a suspect in the precinct. Some kid picked up on some bogus bullshit. Cop pled down and didn't do much time. He probably had some connections."

"So that's what we dealin' with?"

"Also mentioned that the folks don't want to deal with the cops. Afraid the kid might be wiped out if they did. Might be more but that's all I got right now," Jimmy said.

Someone turned up the jukebox even louder, and Ray Charles sang of a rainy night in Georgia. Midway down the bar, an old man snapped his fingers. His other hand rested on the plump thigh of the young woman nestled beside him. "Hey, Jimmy. Tonight I'm celebratin' my sixtieth. What kind of bubbly you hidin' in the cellar?"

His round face glowed in the frosted light and his hair lay across his scalp like thin rivulets of black ink. Jimmy moved toward them, unsure whether the man was celebrating his sixtieth birthday or his sixtieth turn of good luck.

"I got Moët, Pipers, Dom Pee. Chilled. Ready for your special occasion." He smiled at the man and winked at the girl, then returned to the rear and filled a silver wine bucket with ice. He slid two flutes from the overhead rack and picked up a towel. He looked at Marin as he maneuvered. "What I heard ain't much," he whispered, "but I know those guys. They partial to chrome. Their rep is so bad, if they was in the bush, snakes would roll out their way. Watch when you step to 'em."

"See you guys later," Marin said, moving away from the stool. "I got to walk." He paused and looked at Chance. "Solo."

Chance nodded. "I hear you, man."

CHAPTER 22

Day 10, Late Evening

Marin looked at the place on Fifth Avenue near 128th Street and wondered why some folks called it a mansion. It was not as large as Jimmy had described. The house was a three-story sandstone with red turrets and barred windows surrounded by an eight-foot wrought-iron fence. The windows seemed shrouded, and he was not sure if they were covered with dark drapes or simply blacked out. A high gate ornamented with large medieval shields and crossed swords secured the entrance. He stood on the corner diagonally across from the house and looked at the four Dobermans pacing inside the enclosure. They did not bark or leap against the fence but passersby knew enough to be on their guard until they cleared the area.

Marin lit a cigarette, cupping his hand against the glare of the lighter. He glanced at the shields and swords and wondered how far Savoy was trying to run from his Carolina roots or how much he had known of the old Collyer brothers—two eccentric white millionaires who years ago had lived in the cluttered four-story mansion one block away. The Collyer brothers had had enough money to buy half of Harlem, yet had lived without heat or light in a building stacked to the ceiling with tattered newspapers, rusted baby carriages, a half-dozen grand pianos, remnants of an old Model T Ford, discarded radiators, broken furniture, Christmas trees, and colonies of rats that swarmed wild through the debris.

He was too young to remember but for years he had listened to his folks talk about the day the police had hacked their way through the roof to look for the two men. Langley Collyer was found dead in a tunnel of junk, a victim of one of his own booby traps. And Homer Collyer, sick and blind and dependent on Langley for his meals, had died of starvation.

It was rumored that the mansion was haunted, and for years passersby, his folks included, had chosen to walk on the other side of the avenue.

Marin leaned against a mailbox and looked at Savoy's place. The house was sealed against the night and the dogs prowled soundlessly. He watched folks cross to the other side of the avenue or walk in the street to avoid them. The scene with its surrounding enclosure reminded him of a shadowy movie set temporarily thrown together.

. . . *No way of gettin' in. And place ain't on Chance's route, so he ain't gonna get nuthin' from here.*

He flicked the cigarette into the gutter and was about to leave when a side door under the high stoop opened. Two men emerged and the dogs surrounded them in a pack. Their barking could be heard for blocks but they fell silent when one of the men raised his hand and whispered a word. He was slightly built and wore an old-fashioned smoking jacket of paisley silk over a shirt with a knotted tie, and dark pants. Smoke trailed from the cigarette in his hand, and his face, to Marin, was familiar and peculiar. Like a small-mouthed amphibian.

. . . Savoy ain't changed a bit. Still lookin' like the Creature from the Black Lagoon, except the older he get, the uglier he looks.

Savoy opened the gate and Marin let out a breath. Detective Leahy's yellow hair glinted in the streetlight as he walked to a car that had the motor running. Savoy disappeared through the door under the stoop and the car took off. Marin wanted to light another cigarette but the flare of the lighter might attract more attention than he needed. He moved from behind the mailbox and strolled away quickly. Had he glanced over his shoulder, he would have seen another car, parked in the bus stop down the street, pull from the curb and ease away.

The phone was ringing as he walked in and Mama Pat looked up from her knitting.

"How you doin'?" she said. "Margaret just went to sleep so I—"

He put his finger to his mouth to silence her as he lifted the receiver. They both heard the breathing even before he put the phone to his ear. It was heavy, as if someone had rushed to get to him with information he did not want to hear. He waited until Mama Pat went into the bedroom before he spoke.

"Yeah?"

"What the fuck you tryin' to do?"

"Whoa. Who's this? Who's callin'?"

"I'm warnin' you! Keep your ass outta this shit. It don't concern you!"

"Who's givin' me this advice?"

The phone went dead and the buzz of the dial tone resonated in the kitchen.

Mama Pat reemerged with her purse, stared at Marin's face, and sat down again. "What? What's the matter?"

Her eyes arced with fright and she squeezed her pocketbook to her chest as if someone were about to snatch it. "What is it, Marin?"

"Nuthin', Mama Pat. It's probably nuthin'."

She touched his sleeve and he felt the tremor through the fabric. "Marin, are you all right?"

He gazed beyond her to the half-opened door of the bedroom. Margaret lay on her side, her face turned toward the window. In the dim glow of the small lamp, her shoulder rose slightly with each breath. How, he wondered, could he, Margaret, or anything else be all right? It would never be all right. He had to find his baby.

He turned again and hugged Mama Pat. Her heart beat like a bird and he held on as if she might fly away. Finally, he said, "I'm . . . I'm okay. Lemme walk you downstairs. Put you in a cab."

"I can stay if you want . . . "

"No. No. You need some sleep. I'll see you in the morning, okay?"

He watched the cab pull away, then sprinted back upstairs to check on Margaret.

. . . I'm leavin' you alone for the first time but you hold on, baby. Hold on. Everything be all right. Be back before you turn over.

Then he dialed the Fat Man. Jimmy came on against a background of music and noise. Marin kept his voice low. "Listen, is Chance still there?"

"Naw. Said he might be back though."

"If you see 'im, tell 'im I got a stop to make at Sandy's."

"On 140th Street?"

"Yeah."

"That joint's on red alert. You be on the lookout."

"What I'm after ain't gonna take but a quick minute."

"Ain't but a quick minute for shit to go down, you know that," Jimmy said.

Marin hung up and walked back to the bedroom. A warm breeze lifted the curtain at the half-opened window. He adjusted the cover on Margaret's shoulder, eased down to kiss her forehead, then moved silently to the door.

Outside again, he walked fast, hoping to catch up with Clyde, one of the few remaining friends on the block where he had grown up. Everyone else had moved away, died, or had enlisted in the army of the living dead—so strung out, if they had lain down permanently no one would have known the difference.

The whole scene had changed when Marin had returned from Vietnam and, struggling to contain the nightmare of his own experience, he no longer had the capacity to absorb the narrative of someone else's hard life; had no patience to pretend and grin with those few who still hung out, talking loud and saying nothing; still shuckin' on a dime, as Chance liked to say.

Clyde, who liked to call himself an entrepreneur even though he could not spell the word, was still there and dancing on more than a dime. Several dollars, in fact. He was unruffled and imperturbable and into any- and everything that promised to bring a one hundred percent return on his investment.

His "No Questions Asked" policy had made him the man to see but Marin had to be careful. In a sweep, anyone within a mile of Clyde would probably go down with him.

Clyde was sitting on the last stool at the end of the bar when Marin walked in. The music was loud and he did not look up but knew instinctively that someone was at his elbow. He turned in a half circle, laughed, and held out his hand.

"Marin. My man. Ain't seen much of you. What's goin' on?"

"Nuthin' much. I need somethin' . . ."

"Damn. You sure don't beat 'round the bush. Cool a minute."

"Wish I could but I'm jammed. Need a package kinda ASAP."

"Like . . . ?"

Marin glanced around. Folks were tapping to the rhythm of Parliament Funkadelic and the sound was loud enough to make the walls tremble. Couples were doing the bump in the narrow aisle. The door slammed open and a man built like a linebacker strode in and shouted above the noise, "Who the motherfucka I owe that twenty dollars to?"

No one answered. He slapped the bill on the bar and waited. Marin glanced at him, leaned closer to Clyde, and lowered his voice even though he was sure he could not be heard above the fracas.

"I need somethin' hold maybe twelve rounds."

"What you plannin' on spendin'?"

"Tell me what you got?"

"Hi-Power."

"What?"

Clyde rested his elbows against the counter. "Come on. You ain't been off the scene that long. I mean Browning 9s. Been around since Hector but they some trusty-ass pieces. Git the job done. They pushin' all this new shit on the market but my people still spring for the B. So good they call it Hi-Power." Clyde spoke with the casual confidence of a new-car salesman accustomed to his product's selling itself.

Marin rubbed his chin. "Right. Right. That'll do. And I'll need couple boxes of cartridges."

"Heard about your problem. Baby girl gone. Man, that's some tough shit."

"I'm workin' on it, Clyde. Somethin' gonna break real soon."

"Hope so."

Clyde was a medium-built, compact man with a dark, sharp chiseled face, umbrella-wide Afro, and a signature gold incisor that flashed like a warning light whenever he opened his mouth. He was dressed in a black linen shirt, white pants, and five-hundred-dollar custom-made black sandals and no socks. The shirt was open at the neck to display a gold chain with links the size of small sausages.

"Back in a minute," he said. "Have a taste. Take the edge off while you waitin'."

He slid off the stool, signaled to the bartender for his guest, and walked to the front of the bar. The crowd hi-fived him and edged out of his path. The light from the neon sign in the window illuminated the smiling face of a young man who had been hogging the phone as if it were his private line. Clyde tapped him lightly on the shoulder.

"Tell the babe you gotta disconnect. Matta of life and death."

The young man frowned, then recognized Clyde and placed the receiver on the hook without saying good-bye. "I was just about to hang up, man. Sometimes you can't cut these women loose no matter how hard you try. Know what I mean? Some of 'em gotta be let down easy-like."

Clyde was not interested in face-saving. He did not answer and dialed quickly, his back to the man. When he returned to his seat, Marin had finished the drink he had offered.

"Need this tonight, right?"

"First thing."

"Give it twenty minutes. Stuff got to percolate . . ."

When the package arrived, Clyde, true to his rep, asked no questions but surprised Marin by refusing to take his money. Instead he pressed his fist to Marin's shoulder.

"This on me. Got a kid myself. You remember Marie? Baby girl look like I spit her out. She eighteen now and the first one in the family to see inside a college classroom. Last summer some nig-nog 'round the block with three kids from three different women had Marie in his crosshairs. Girl out of class for the summer and he schemin' to add another notch to his dick. Me and my boys put him in quick check; jacked his ass up so tight he ain't broke wind for a month. For insurance, I transferred my baby girl on down to a college in Delaware. Drove her there myself. Outta state but not outta sight. If somebody lay a finger, soon as I git the wire, they be Dee-Eee-Dee. Dead.

He looked at Marin in the dim light and sucked his teeth. "Shit, man. You and me, we old school. Go way back. Remember them fifty-cent pickup games we used to play? I wasn't no taller then than I am now but you took time out to show me the right play, schooled me how to win.

"And remember them dances at the Y after the games? Chicks hangin' us like we just hit the number or sumthin'. Called us Slim and Shorty, the Deadly Duo, back in the day. Sometimes when I'm coolin' solo, listenin' to some old eight-tracks, I think on them days."

He watched Marin handle the package, then step into the bathroom. When he emerged, Clyde said, "When you catch a breath, we gotta sit and talk some serious shit, but right now, you wadin' through some hip-deep stuff. And you gotta do the right thing."

Marin closed the door on the noise and music and retraced his steps toward Fifth Avenue. The Browning rested smoothly under his shirt against the small of his back, and he carried three small boxes of cartridges in a plastic bag.

Hi-power. He had forgotten about that because its weight was nothing compared to what he had strapped on in 'Nam. Some nights before the unit went out, he had grabbed every weapon they had issued. He was togged down: a .45, an M-16, a Bowie strapped to his ankle, and a bandolier so heavy he felt as if another person had hitched a ride on his chest.

In the fluid darkness, he had fantasized that the weight was a woman's weight, Margaret's weight, and that had kept him pumped up, ready for whatever was crouching in the midnight beyond the next hill.

He crossed Lenox Avenue thinking of the bandolier and decided he didn't need it. It would have only slowed him. The conflagration in Southeast Asia had not been a war in the conventional sense. He understood that as soon as he had stepped off the transport. In the heat of that jungle, basic training took a walk and basic instinct took up residence. It was hide, hit, and get the hell on out.

. . . Run, duck, crawl, swim with a fuckin' alligator if we had to . . . and sometimes it was just plain luck. Me and Chance, we was lucky. Some of our guys, all we found was strips of skin. We couldn't send that back.

He strolled past the Club Baron and heard the music and glanced at the crowd waiting in line. He listened to their laughter and tried not to think about what he and Margaret might be doing if this craziness had not dropped into the middle of their lives. He drew in a breath and the air, less humid, entered his lungs and lent a coolness to the night that steadied him. He walked in long strides and the weapon fit against him as if it were molded there.

. . . Tap the bell on the top of the gate near those swords. If things don't go right, Hi-Power'll take care of the dogs and then say hello to Savoy.

Fifth Avenue at one A.M. was empty. What traffic there was moved fast in an effort to beat the light at 125th Street. If they were lucky enough to catch it on yellow, they kept going, speeding around the curve of Garvey Park before slowing to a leisurely crawl on the other Fifth Avenue, relaxed, the specter of beggars and squeegees no longer visible in the rearview mirror.

Marin approached the gate and stopped when he heard the door under the stoop creak open. There were only two dogs in the yard and they rose to their feet instantly but did not bark. Marin stepped into the shadow of the adjoining building and recognized the Enforcer. He twisted his keys in his hand and moved past Marin toward a black Cadillac parked three cars away.

He leaned over, but before he opened the door, Marin eased up behind him.

"Say!"

The Enforcer spun around and his hand went to his hip, but Marin had drawn his own weapon.

"Don't try it, motherfucka!"

"This a stickup?"

"Not unless you want it to be," Marin whispered. "Turn around."

He pressed his weapon against the Enforcer's ear, pushing him against the car, then removed a snub-nosed .38 from his waistband.

"Now let's talk. Where's my kid?"

"Your what? Man, that was a couple years ago. I did my time, your boy sued, and he ended up with a couple hundred thou. That's squashed. Why you hasslin' me now?"

"Different daddy, this time."

"Look, either you talkin' through your hat or you talkin' to the wrong man."

"I'm talkin' to you and I'm crazy and I got two pieces aimed at your ass! Where's my baby? My daughter?"

"Ooahh . . ." The Enforcer tried to laugh but the sound came out in a ragged groan. His face held a sheen that made his skin look like glass. "I don't believe this fuckin' shit."

"You don't?" Marin pressed both weapons closer and cocked the hammer on his own. The sound was loud in the night air. "You want me to make it real?"

"No, no, no, man! No. Looka here. I'm bein' straight with you. I don't know nuthin' about no baby. Where you comin' from with this?"

"I'm askin' the questions here and I want some answers. Not some fuckin' bullshit."

"I'm *bein'* straight. I don't know what the fuck you talkin' about, man."

"What about your partner?"

"You got to ax him. Whatever's goin' down, leave me outta this shit. I don't know nuthin'."

"Let's walk."

"Where?"

"Back where you came from. You walkin' me past them dogs."

"Man, I'm tellin' you. You bitin' off more than you can chew . . ."

"And you worried about me chokin'? Fuck you! Let's move. I'm gettin' me some answers tonight."

They moved, but not quite together. Marin stayed a step behind, both weapons trained on the Enforcer's spine as they walked toward the gate. He caught the odor of raw sweat in the still air.

The Enforcer raised his hand to ring the bell when Marin heard the sound, like a *thwup*, a single round fired through a silencer from a distance that found its mark.

The thrust of the bullet spun the Enforcer around. He leaned against the gate as if he were resting; then whatever had been holding him together drained away all at once and he sagged to his knees. His eyes were still open, large with surprise. The red bubbled through the hole in his neck and spread down his yellow shirt in a dark triangle.

Behind the gate the dogs crouched on their haunches, the sleek fur on the ridge of their backs stiffened with fright, and they howled, chronicling the presence of death.

Marin dropped behind the car, then slid to the ground and lay on his stomach. He dug into the grit of the pavement with his elbows and inched away. The howling filled his ears but it was the only sound. No getaway squeal of tires, no running feet, no window slammed. Someone, somewhere, was waiting, poised with another bullet.

Marin slid like a snake except there was no high grass, only the metal of parked cars. He wished he had the bandolier with the un-limited rounds but what he had would have to do. Near the corner, he scrambled on elbows and knees and tumbled into a small lot filled with the rusted hulks of abandoned autos and waist-high weeds rank with the smell of damp earth. His sweat was icy and his fingers were locked on both triggers.

A car moved down the side street and he watched it slow down at the light. It was a gypsy cab and idled long enough for him to make a crouching run for the door and dive inside. The driver caught sight of the guns and threw his hands in the air, palms up.

"Wha' happenin'? Aye. Aye. Aye, Brudda . . . Me ain't make no coin yet. Just now pull out the garage, me."

The man stared wide-eyed and raised his arms higher. "Take car, you want it. Me ain't no fighter, no!"

"No, man! Listen! It ain't like that. Here's a ten up front. Take me to the viaduct."

"Where that?"

"A hundred and fifty-fifth Street and St. Nick."

The cabbie blinked and his hands came down. He was shaking but steadied himself enough to snatch the bill. When he put his foot to the pedal, Fifth, then Lenox Avenue, flashed in a ribbon of blinking streetlights and darkened houses. He cut to the right onto Seventh Avenue, where the bars and clubs hung together in a stream of blind-ing luminescence and solitary strollers were caught in frozen tableaux.

"Me got kids. Got kids, man. Got kids."

Marin leaned forward and tapped him on the shoulder. "Be cool. This ain't no stickup. Just git me where I got to go without all the sing-along."

They sped past the Flash Inn at 155th Street and veered left onto the viaduct. Marin stepped out at St. Nicholas Avenue and gave him another five. He slammed the door and watched as the cabbie screeched through a red light. He waited across the avenue from the

156

Fat Man until the cab disappeared. The bar was crowded and he heard the music from where he stood but decided against going inside.

. . . Take a pass tonight. Cabbie probably dimein' me right now. Blue-and-Whites pull up before I turn around. Street too damn hot.

He held up his hand and another cab pulled to the curb. This time the weapons were tucked beneath his shirt and the driver took his time.

Marin slouched in the back seat, too light-headed to reconstruct the recent events. Where had the bullet come from? Had the shooter gotten a look at him? Did this have anything to do with his baby? Why didn't Savoy come out when he heard the dogs?

He thought about the dogs and drew in a breath. Most black folks right away recognized the difference between a howl and a bark. Recognized the message clear enough to make them hug themselves in prayer and contemplate which black dress or suit would need brushing off.

"This shit gettin' thicker by the minute and I'm no closer to finding—"

The cabbie glanced at him in the mirror.

"You say somethin'?"

Marin spoke to the back of his head. "Sorry, man. Just thinkin' out loud."

The cab moved down the viaduct and Marin stared out the window at the spot where he had fought for his life and ended another's. He wondered about the man who had stabbed him and run away. And he wondered—when he had jumped in that cab near Savoy's place—why he had needed to come back here.

When he arrived home, he eased the key in the door. The apartment was quiet except for Margaret's light breathing.

CHAPTER 23

Day 11, 3 A.M.

*I*n the kitchen, Marin lit a cigarette and paced the floor, by turns numb with apprehension, then trembling with fatigue but too wound up to close his eyes. Where had the shot come from? He had been inches away from the Enforcer.

. . . Shooter was a marksman. Had to be. And damn sure was on top of his game.

He paced in the dark, smoking his way through the

pack of Pall Malls. Through the half-opened bedroom door, he heard the creak of the bed as Margaret turned over. She whispered his name in her sleep but he was too afraid to go to her, afraid of her waking and shrinking from the thick smell of fear that had saturated his clothes and the fright that stained his face.

He sat down at the table, immobilized, and watched through the window as dawn inched over the roof, turning indefinable contours gray, then pink. He smoked and listened to the small scattered cry of birds.

Later, he watched sunlight tint the brickwork of the buildings across the courtyard in golden red. It streamed through the kitchen window and painted everything a clear, bright yellow.

He roused himself, emptied the overflowing ashtray, and turned the radio on the windowsill above the sink to WLIB, hoping to get news of the shooting. But the news segment had just ended and Eddie O'Jay was jamming on "Soul at Sunrise."

Fatigue crept in. He wanted to close his eyes and meditate to the hoarse melancholy of Otis Redding, but the sound cut through him like a rusted razor and he snapped the radio off.

In the bathroom, the image in the mirror made him step back. The clothing he had crawled on the sidewalk in seemed not to belong to him. The T-shirt was stained a muddy red and his pants were caked and shredded at the knees. The acrid odor of his sweat stung his nose and the palms of his hands were mottled with dried blood.

He stripped quickly, stuffed the clothing in a plastic bag, and stepped into a scalding shower. When he stepped out, he was still fatigued but clean.

The phone rang, shaking him, but he picked it up on the first ring.

"Yeah?"

"Hey. I guess you got the wire," Chance said. His voice sounded hollow, as if he had not slept or had just woken up. It was nearly 6 A.M. and Chance was an early riser, even on his day off.

"What wire? What's goin' on?"

"Enforcer ain't enforcin' no more," Chance said. "Got his lights put out."

Marin felt his hand shaking and grasped the receiver to hold it steady. He thought of several possible replies but finally said, "Well, everybody knew the guy's pedigree. Got what was comin' to him and not soon enough, if you ask me."

"Well, what—"

"Look, Mama Pat and Naomi will be here in about an hour. I got to get stuff together. I'll be in Miss Adelaide's around nine. I could use a good cup of coffee."

Before Chance could ask another question, Marin hung up, then tiptoed to the bedroom. The doctor had cut Margaret's medication in half and she now slept less, but when he whispered her name, she only turned over and settled into a more comfortable position. She lay on her back, her arm flung over her forehead. Marin leaned against the open door, watching her for several minutes, listening in the stillness, then eased the door closed again.

He was dressed by the time he heard the footsteps on the stairs. They were soft and slow and he knew it was Mama Pat. He opened the door as she was reaching for her key. Naomi followed her inside.

"You got the papers yet?" Mama Pat said, pulling a rolled copy of the *Daily Challenge* from her bag. "Shame about that cop but I always say, what goes 'round comes around."

Marin thought of the note that Tanya's sister, Eunice, had left at the door and wondered if the girl had ever stopped crying. He spread the paper on the dinette table and stared at the headline.

161

At 2 A.M. last night, the quiet of Fifth Avenue and 128th Street was shattered by a bullet that found its mark in the body of thirty-nine-year-old Austen Brown, a former police officer who once served time in prison for sexually assaulting a young male suspect in his custody.

That incident had taken place in an unmarked police car in the precinct parking lot, and the testimony of two eyewitnesses helped send Brown, a ten-year veteran of the department, to prison. He was released two years ago after serving one-third of a ten-year sentence.

The youth's family filed a lawsuit against the NYPD and reached an out-of-court settlement for an undisclosed sum but a crime of this nature is not easily forgotten. Sources speculate that Brown's killing may have been motivated by revenge.

Police say there was no indication of robbery; however, they are investigating a number of leads.

"A number of leads," Marin said, closing the paper. "Same old, same old when they don't know nuthin'."

"Might be revenge. Just like they say," Naomi whispered. She peered in on Margaret and then left the door ajar.

"I see you goin' out," Mama Pat said. "What's in the bag?"

"Garbage."

"Well, while you out, mind pickin' up some things? Not much. Just some shampoo, some baking powder, and some tomato sauce. I forgot those."

"We gonna fix red rice, collard greens, crisp fried chicken, and do up some cornbread that'll make your mouth water," Naomi said. She was standing in front of the cupboard, pulling out bowls and pots and pans, and Marin held his breath, hoping he had placed the weapons on a shelf high enough and too far out of her reach.

He had no appetite but took the list. He wanted to tell them that it was too hot to be baking anything. The kitchen itself already felt like an oven, even though it was not yet eight o'clock and the fan was on high speed.

But cornbread. He couldn't remember the last time he'd tasted a slice with thick crust and the butter oozing out the middle. Too many things had gotten in the way, too much pain had warped the rhythm of their lives.

. . . There should be jars of baby food in that cupboard. There should be formula. And baby bottles.

He tried to concentrate as Mama Pat went on. "Margaret likes bein' in the kitchen," she said. "She's helpin' now instead of just sittin' and watchin'. This is good for her. Prayer and food—good food—will help you work through a lot of problems."

He nodded and leaned over to kiss her on the forehead. "Mama Pat, how about some ice cream to go along with that?"

"Fine with me," Naomi cut in. "Strawberry for me, chocolate for Mama, and butter pecan for Margaret. Her appetite's almost back and you know she's gotta make up for lost time."

Outside in the hall, Marin thought of "lost time." Too much time had already passed. Detective Benjamin had not contacted him since he'd asked him to forget about that note. Last night, the slim lead had ended up with a bullet in his neck and the other, the Fireplug, had probably skipped town already, afraid that somebody might be gunning for him too.

He glanced at the list and walked down the stairs. Then he doubled back and banged on the door. Naomi opened it and stared at him. "What? What's wrong?"

"Uh, look. I just want to remind you. I got my key so if anybody rings, don't answer the door. Not for anybody, okay?"

"Okay, but—"

"I . . . I just want to make sure everything's—"

Naomi shook her head. "Marin, what's wrong?"

"Nothing. Nothing. Just close the door and lock it. I'll be back in a minute."

Fifteen minutes later, he returned with the package. "If Chance calls, tell 'im I'm on my way. We'll be in Miss Adelaide's."

Mama Pat turned from the stove to shake her head. "Now don't you fill up on that woman's food when you got good home cookin' right here. Margaret's gettin' ready, so don't be gone too long."

He heard the splash of the shower in the bathroom and knew that Margaret was up, probably unsteady on her feet, probably crying as she gazed in the mirror trying to prepare herself to face another day filled with unanswered prayers. He wondered if he should step in there, help her.

He imagined her standing before the clouded mirror naked and wet. If he had been here alone with her, he would have stepped in, pressed her to him. He thought of the feeling that would well up inside him. His jaw began to ache and he felt the pressure of his grinding teeth. Something from somewhere somehow had to fall his way. A name. A place. Something.

. . . *Fireplug. If he's still in town, I'll find his ass. If he turns up cold, I'll break in on Savoy. He knows something. Shoot every last one of those dogs if I have to.*

He watched Mama Pat and Naomi busy themselves at the counter. They had been here for half an hour and so far no one had mentioned the baby. Maybe they had talked while he was at the store. Maybe they'd talk some more while Margaret helped with the cooking. Maybe this was what she needed.

He looked at Mama Pat and nodded: "I'm only goin' for coffee. Only coffee."

———

Miss Adelaide's restaurant was on the corner of 146th Street and Eighth Avenue next door to the Trelawny West Indian Bakery. Miss Adelaide's screen door not only kept the flies out but allowed the aroma of her cooking to drift out, and at times this pulled in more people than she could accommodate.

She was a thin dark woman of sixty who had papered the walls in her favorite pale blue, and the half-dozen tables were set up each morning with white linen cloths and vases of cut flowers. Cafe curtains diffused the light from the street and fluttered in the breeze when the door opened.

She did all the cooking; used real butter in her baking, real sugar in the iced tea, and folks learned to be patient because she made everything from scratch and did not skimp on the servings. This also kept the place crowded.

It was hard not to move beyond the cup of coffee and the pyramid of buttermilk biscuits but Marin knew what was waiting for him at home. He leaned back and ordered a second cup while Chance worked through the plate of grits and fried whiting. They sat at a small table in the corner near the window, and Marin watched passersby as Chance spoke.

"So one is down. Out the picture," he whispered. "That ain't the end of the game. Been askin' some of the guys on the other routes. They heard of Fireplug. One of 'em thinks he has a room in a walk-up somewhere on Sugar Hill, 156th Street or thereabouts. One block from Riverside Drive." He looked in Marin's face and paused. "This only a rumor, not a fact."

"That'll do," Marin said. "I take care of the rest."

Chance lifted his cup, then put it down. "I stopped by Sandy's last night. Clyde said I'd just missed you . . ."

"Yeah? What'd you do?"

"Nothin' much. Drove around a bit thinkin' maybe I'd catch up to you."

Marin looked out of the window across the avenue at the Harlem Gardens, the corner bar. The place was not yet open and he watched the maintenance man maneuver a hose over the pavement to flush bits of litter into the street. A small rainbow arced in the mist above the water.

Not many people were out strolling and he guessed it was because of the temperature. Too hot to do anything. Two girls, teenagers, turned the corner carrying large straw bags and rolled towels under their arms, heading for the pool on Bradhurst Avenue. One held her swim cap in her hand. Both were laughing at something.

Marin turned back to gaze at Chance.

"So you only drove around. Where'd you end up?"

"Fat Man. 'Round two o'clock. Nothin' much was happenin' so I made it on home."

Marin nodded. "Know where I was?"

Chance pushed his plate away and folded his arms on the table. "Lemme guess."

Marin remained silent and Chance's eyes widened.

"Shit, Marin. You took 'im out?"

"Hell no. And keep your voice down. I barely got outta the way. Shot come from somewhere across the street. I was a half-step behind the mark when he went down. Got the hell outta there fast as I could. Before he got hit though, we had words. He swore he didn't know what I was talkin' about. I was walkin' him to the gate, to get me past the dogs to Savoy when he went down . . ."

"So who you think?"

"Damn if I know, but whoever it was had an appointment and wanted to keep it quiet. Used a silencer."

"Shit. The other one probably on the run right now. Everybody plus his mama know Fireplug got tissue paper for brains, but dumb or not, he gotta know the signs when he see 'em. Probably brakin' for gas at the Maryland state line as we speak."

Miss Adelaide walked over and slipped another platter of biscuits on the table. Her hair was covered in an indigo scarf and her dark skin was seamless. "How my favorite fellas doin'? I'm still prayin' for you, Marin. You hold on."

"Thanks, Miss Adelaide. I really appreciate that."

Marin watched Chance reach for another biscuit, his fourth, and wondered where all the food was going. He had not gained a pound since the day they first met.

Five years ago. Vietnam. He had burst out of the commissary and stood in the dusty clearing, cursing so loud everyone, including Marin, had turned to watch.

Three white officers had also stopped and one strode toward him. Marin walked faster and got to Chance first.

"Say, brother. What's goin' on?"

"Cracker motherfucka behind the counter heard I'd got a medal and asked me where I bought it from," Chance said. He was trembling with anger and his face was wet with sweat. "I told 'im I ain't had to buy my medal. I got it from his mama for her appreciation of my services. He ain't like that and want to go at it. I told 'im I be waitin' outside. If he come out, they gonna be shippin' his rebel white ass home in pieces."

Marin looked at the approaching officer, scanned the knife crease of his uniform, the buzz cut so fresh his scalp showed raw and pink. His face, not yet roughened by heat, dirt, and fear, was like a marshmallow. He was, Marin guessed, a newly arrived second looey, not anxious to get the muck of Vietnam on his hands just yet. He marched with the authority of West Point imprinted in his stride, but to Marin he appeared stiff-legged, as if he'd already been injured. Marin saluted sharply and stepped to him.

"Sir, a misunderstanding. We can work it out."

The officer did not acknowledge the salute, but stared at Chance. "Get yourself cleaned up, soldier."

He turned his back and Marin watched him stroll over to the other officers, heard the laugh at a whispered comment as they moved on.

"And fuck you too," Marin breathed.

"See what I mean," Chance said. "All these fuckin' crackerjacks can go straight to hell, no detour."

Marin touched his shoulder. Chance's fatigues were caked with dirt and he smelled as if he hadn't seen a shower in a month. His unit had just returned to base. Through the mud on the jacket, Marin was able to read the patch WATKINS.

He shook a cigarette from his pack and held the pack toward Watkins. "Where you from?"

"You mean stateside?"

"Yeah."

"Harlem, USA."

"Hey. I'm Taylor, Marin Taylor. Grew up on 140th near Seventh. I'm on 148th now."

"Well, I'll be damned." Chance held out his hand. "How come we ain't never run into each other? I used to hang in Basie's Lounge, sometimes in Thelma's on Seventh, but most of the times I be down in Minton's. That's my spot. Name's Watkins, Chance Watkins."

Chance's platoon had been in the field for three weeks and had sustained heavy casualties. The remaining soldiers, those few who had returned to base, were being absorbed into Marin's unit. The injured were going to Japan or Okinawa. The dead were being shipped to Dover Air Base, in Delaware.

"This ain't about winnin' no war," Chance said later that night. They sat hunched over a smoky lantern on the perimeter of the base and squinted into the surrounding darkness. The air was thick with mosquitoes and they were afraid to open their mouths too often for fear that some would fly in. The smoke from the lantern did not help and the flickering light only drew more. The insects came in waves out of the wet night. The skin cream the men were issued seemed to serve as an appetizer so Chance threw it away and relied on alcohol, the home remedy his mother's folks had used when she was a girl.

Chance rubbed his arms, face, and the nape of his neck with vodka to soothe the swelling from the bites.

"This shit is about politics," he said. "Nobody talkin' about what's happenin' stateside. Those kids at Kent State and Jackson State college. Shot 'em down in the street like dogs. Just like dogs.

"We hearin' all this feel-good stuff about body counts but they ain't tellin' folks the true facts. We on the ground and know the deal. I say, hell with all that John Wayne take-it-to-the-top bullshit. Only action he ever seen was probably in somebody's Hollywood bed. If he was lucky. So main thing I'm doin' here is tryin' to survive, save my ass. That's it."

"What about that bronze star?" Marin said. "Few hours ago, you was ready to beat that cracker's ass down to the ground because of it."

Chance peered at Marin in the dim light and raised his hand. "Lemme say somethin', man. This medal don't mean shit. I mean how many jobs this medal gonna get me once we back in the world?"

He poured more vodka onto a handkerchief and spread it across his chest.

"Under fire, I damn sure wasn't thinkin' about no medal. You in a spot, you do what you got to do. I lifted those two guys and dragged 'em fifty yards back to the medics. They was able to put one back together, but the other, the white kid, kicked off before they could pump the needle in his arm. Shrapnel had come right though the helmet and out the other side. The helmet was the only thing holding his head on. Only nineteen years old."

He looked away into the dark, listening intently, as if he might have heard something apart from the familiar nocturnal noise. A second passed before he turned back to Marin. "When I get back in the world, I'm gonna contact that kid's family somehow, let 'em know that he was an okay son, brother, father. Whatever. Least I can do. But right now, I say this: You watch my back. I watch yours. And we just might kick luck's ass and make it back together . . ."

"We just might," Marin said. He had taken the bottle and splashed the alcohol on his arms. He felt the insects, some as large and long as his fingers, retreat and return seconds later, larger and hungrier.

He imagined they brought their family, friends, neighbors to chew away

*larger pieces of his skin. They were like an invading army, made bold by
their numbers.*

*Why were he and Chance ordered to sit out here in the first place? To lis-
ten for what? If the V.C. had been near enough, they could have slid up on
them and slit their throats in the time it took to turn around. And he and
Chance would not have heard a twig snap or a blade of grass move.*

*He eyed the bottle again. It was three-quarters empty, but he knew they
had another so he splashed more of the alcohol on his arms. He felt a slight
respite as the insects retreated. He used the moment to open his mouth and
pour the rest down his throat.*

The restaurant had gotten crowded but was still quiet except
for the small radio on the shelf behind the counter. Gladys
Knight was singing above the low murmur.

Marin reached for another biscuit and wondered how he and
Chance had managed to make it back from 'Nam at all. They had
gone through all that hell and had made it home, free of visible
wounds, but all that scar tissue was inside, growing thick as snakes.
And it grew as time passed, feeding on memories that refused to die.

He wanted to lose himself in the sound of Gladys Knight but he
couldn't. He was thinking of last night, of the shooter with the silencer, and felt the reptiles once again stirring in his gut.

CHAPTER 24

Day 11, 10 A.M.

*C*hance drove up the hill at 145th Street, and Marin scanned the passersby, particularly watching every woman who pushed a baby carriage. Then he glanced at his watch. They drove past Convent Avenue Baptist Church and turned onto Amsterdam Avenue and Marin glanced at his watch again.

"You got an appointment?" Chance said.

"Just that I promised to be back in time for dinner and—"

"Dinner. We just left the restaurant from breakfast."

They drove north, past sidewalks crowded with vendors and people shopping for fruits and vegetables. Outside the stores, people searched through bins of kitchenware, sneakers, blouses, and stacks of vintage records. Music from the ice-cream cart competed with sound blaring from the restaurants and travel agencies.

Chance's eyes flitted away from the traffic long enough to regard Marin's face. Marin's mouth was a thin twisted seam held together as if something inside were struggling to break out.

"Look Marin, say the word and we head back. I drop you home. We can scout Plug some other time."

"No. No. Blew too much time already. Let's see his hangout. I got to think about—"

A scream of tires behind them sent Chance swerving to the curb. His foot jammed the brakes as a cruiser flew past—no lights, no siren.

"What the hell is this? Fuckin' Blue-and-Whites act like they own the damn road."

They watched buses screech to a halt, pedestrians sprint to the curb, and other cars veer out of the way as more cruisers sped past, this time with sirens and lights. Traffic was at a standstill, and Chance leaned on the wheel, trying to peer ahead. "Think we gotta hike it. The Man has set up shop and the scene is closed down. We got to foot it."

Three blocks away a noisy crowd milled in the street watching the police, who stood near the barricades trying to ignore them. A photographer loaded his camera with more film and angled a long shot at the lobby door of the corner building while a team of plainclothesmen stood in a tight knot, smoking cigarettes and watching him.

Three officers removed flak jackets, placed them in a van, then stood, scowling red-faced in the noon sun, also ignoring the catcalls. Marin and Chance edged through the crowd to lean against the barricade, and Marin nudged a short, heavy man standing near him sucking on a toothpick. "What happened?"

"Dope deal. Cat got wasted."

"Who was it?"

"Some guy went for bad. They say he pulled his piece. Wasn't fast enough. Chest got more fresh air than he could take."

"Yeah?"

"Yep. Cops pop first and ax questions later."

The fat man chewed on the toothpick, then curled it in his mouth and spit it out. "Anyway, that's how they claim it went down," he said. "I ain't nobody's eyewitness."

Marin shaded his eyes against the sun and tried to make out the figure sprawled halfway in the lobby door. The man lay face down in the hallway, one foot visible on the top step of the stoop.

A thin man in a postal uniform squeezed between the barricade, nodded to Marin, and tapped Chance on the shoulder. "What's happenin'? Y'all takin' in a little Sugar Hill action?"

"Hey, Parker. Ain't seen you in a while. You don't hang in the Fat Man anymore?"

"Not right now. You know everybody snatchin' vacation what with the kids outta school so I'm catchin' this overtime while I can. Be back when things slow down."

"Who's that took the bullet?"

"Some lightweight supposed to be one of Savoy's musclemen," Parker said. His skin was splotched red from the weather and his gray postal shirt had wet circles under the arms. He shifted his mail sack from one shoulder to the other and added, "And you know, that other one got it in the neck last night."

Marin glanced at Chance, then at Parker again. "That one up there, that's the one they call Fireplug? That's who's stretched out?"

"You got it. Look like Savoy doin' a little spring cleanin'. I catch y'all later. Maybe at the Fat Man on a slow night."

The crowd was growing larger, tighter, and louder. Parker moved away. Marin turned and edged back through the crowd and the rising catcalls. He could feel a different kind of heat and wondered when the first spark would catch, then flame into something that ended in more bodies, a curfew, and the rumble of National Guard Jeeps.

Chance followed him to the perimeter, where they both halted. Several yards away, Leahy sat behind the wheel of a black Cadillac smoking a cigarette. He wore a khaki shirt and black slacks and his arm rested on the open door. His hair was slick against his scalp and his face was in profile as he squinted into the white sun.

"There's our boy," Marin said.

He watched the detective inhale and trail the smoke through his thin nostrils, watched him squint one eye to study the wisps as if they held secrets that were blowing away too fast for him to read.

CHAPTER 25

Day 11, Noon

Conroy ruffled the paper and then spread it out.

"Oh shit!" He slammed the pages down on the milk crate that served as his table and jumped up from the stool.

At the sound, his mother came into the room, weaving her way around the piles of boxes.

"What happened? Why you usin' all that language? I told you about that."

She leaned against the door, waiting, with her arms folded.

"Yeah, yeah, Ma. Look. One of the guys that beat me up got iced. Somebody took care of 'im."

He hugged himself, laughed, and began to move around in the small space he had cleared. "Oh man, I wish I coulda been the one to done it. All the stuff they put on me, I wish I coulda been the one."

"But you ain't, so now what? What you intend to do? One got canceled but what you owe Savoy is still on the books. Long as he operatin', you in trouble. Look, why don't you at least try and get a nine-to-five, then go to him and explain how you gonna pay a little every week. It ain't gonna—"

"Ma, I told you, it don't work like that. A little a week is chump change, don't even cover his vigorish."

"His what?"

"His interest. It doubles by the day, know what I mean? I need to clean this up all at one time. Don't leave nuthin' hangin', you understand?"

The old woman eased into a chair opposite him. Her brow was seamed more from fatigue than age and her hands shook as she fumbled with the buttons on her sweater. She had gone out at 4 A.M. to scavenge a few bottles and cans, then stopped in the all-night deli where they knew her and she was able to trade the empties for two containers of coffee. The owner, an old Dominican man, sold her a quarter-pound of cheese and salami and two buttered rolls, put it on her tab, then told his son to walk with her to the corner and watch as she walked down the street to her building.

She had gone back out later to buy the newspaper because Conroy would probably want to know what was going on in the world. There was no electricity and the batteries for the portable radio had died. With no gas, most of her small Social Security check went for takeout food, and her check wasn't due for another two weeks.

She had been holding on, managing all right until he had come creeping back two nights ago, complaining he'd had no place to stay;

had got put out because his woman, who he thought loved him, had taken up with somebody else.

She had looked at him through narrow eyes and shrugged. "That somebody probably got a job, I hope. No point in the girl goin' from bad to worse."

The remark had set him off, and she watched him stomp into the small bedroom, except there was no bed, only more garbage, which he threw into the living room, adding still more obstacles to maneuver around. He crouched on the floor and finally curled up in a moth-eaten blanket. She knew he intended to sleep until she got tired of talking, blaming him for Tito's death, and how she would have been out of this firetrap long ago if her beloved son were still here to handle things.

Tito's gone and I have nothing. Nothing. Now here's more trouble. How long will it be before Savoy finds where Conroy's hiding? Before he probably set fire to the place, burn us out into the open, and make him cough up what he owes. Lord, what am I to do?

Conroy had kept the window open so that the street sounds almost balanced out the wailing. Today, however, he could ignore her completely. The Enforcer had been exed out of the picture, and night had turned to day.

He put the paper down and reached for his T-shirt, his head swimming with plans.

. . . Gotta make some fast moves. Git dressed. Make it on over to the Salvation Army and pick up some grub. Hear from the street what really went down. Enforcer iced. Ain't that somethin'. Like the paper say, probably payback for what he done that time to that kid. Where the fuck is Fireplug? He still around, means I still got to watch my back but I ain't got to hole up in a cave like some damn vampire. Can move 'round a whole lot more.

He waited until his mother left the room before he reached under the sagging chair to retrieve a small plastic bag. He held it up, then pulled out each piece to examine again.

. . . Unload some of this jewelry. Thelma think she could junk me, but I wish I could hear what she got to say now. Probably bent way outta shape over these ivory necklaces. Shit. All I heard was her braggin' how she brought 'em back all the way from Africa. The motherland. Fuck that. Look who got 'em now, and I ain't been no further than the Bronx. What the hell. Hooked all ten of her dead mama's bracelets while I was at it. These is old gold. Each one eighteen karats.

He enfolded them in the tissue and placed the bag under the sofa again.

. . . Maybe I shop 'em one at a time. That'll keep me on my feet till I find Sadie. She and that kid someplace close. Spread some dollars around, somethin' bound to come up. It always do.

The line outside the Salvation Army center was longer than usual, which meant he might hear more than the usual talk. He tuned out the stuff everyone had heard yet still loved to tell: worn tales of bad luck, hard luck, missed luck, no luck at all. He wanted to step away but not so far as to miss something that might be important.

Overhead, the sun was white in a slate blue cloudless sky, and he wished he had worn a hat. The line of people moved one step at a time and he moved with them. There was no breeze to relieve the heat rising like a current from the pavement. He was the third person from the entrance when he heard something that made him step off the line.

He looked behind him, then approached the two men. One was about his height but more pumped up. His face held the artificial brightness sometimes seen on just-released-from-Riker's men not yet accustomed to breathing free air. The other man was medium height with a bulging torso and bloodshot eyes that seemed to look everywhere except at the person he was speaking to. In the noon sun his skin was dry and flaky, as if he had not seen a shower or bath in some time.

"What's happenin'?" Conroy said.

"Nuthin' much," the pumped one said. "What's goin' on with you?"

The other one remained silent but they both eyed him, took quick inventory of his too-large T-shirt and soiled, wrinkled chinos and decided he was as broke as they were, with nothing worth stealing.

Conroy shrugged. "Heard y'all mention a name sound a little familiar, that's all . . ."

"You mean Fireplug?"

"Yeh."

"You know him?" The man's bloodshot eyes danced, and then seemed to settle on something that might have been floating an inch to the left of Conroy's ear. Conroy was tempted to turn around and follow his gaze but decided against it.

"I sorta know him," Conroy said. "Ran across him one time in a after-hours spot. Saw him and his ace perpetrate some real shady shit."

The two men laughed and slapped hands. "They can forgit shady and everything else," the pumped one said. "Enforcer got paid last night and Plug got his ass unplugged 'bout an hour ago."

They said this as the line inched toward the entrance. The door yawned open, and at the smell of food, the two rushed inside, forgetting about Conroy.

He remained where he was, blinking in the sun, waiting for someone else to come up behind him and tap him on the shoulder and whisper that it was all a joke.

. . . Or maybe a trap. Spread a rumor that would draw him out. But what if it was true? The real deal. What now?

The line moved past him but he ignored it.

. . . *How this shit happen? Probably turf war. Somebody beamin' in on Savoy's landscape.*

He grinned, imagining Savoy lying low, trying to regroup, hustle up replacements. "He gonna need it. Left and right hand cut off in less than twenty-four hours. Whole lotta shit done hit and it's too late to duck."

Euphoria overcame fear, hunger evaporated, and he turned to walk back to his mother's place. He moved slowly, reveling in the lopsided, cocky strut that once more informed his stroll.

CHAPTER 26

Day 11, 3 P.M.

"What I can't understand is how that shitty excuse for a cop is all over the place." Marin blew out a breath trying to expel the familiar anger he felt each time he saw the detective. "I mean, he's down on Fifth. He cruises the strip. Now he's up here on the hill sittin' ringside at a public rubout.

"Maybe he's posin' as the Vanilla Avenger. Got a monopoly on crime-fightin'," Chance said. "Or maybe NYPD just shorthanded. You know a good cop is hard to find these days, especially in Harlem."

"Shee-it!"

Chance did not respond but wove through the traffic until they reached the viaduct. Marin again stared at the spot where he had fought for his life. He wondered again what had happened to the dead man's brother, the one called Conroy. He also wondered why Detective Benjamin had not returned any of his calls.

At Seventh Avenue, Chance made a right turn and slowed down. He cruised toward the Flash Inn, then eased to a stop near the canopied entrance.

"You down for a taste?"

"No. No. Gotta see what's happenin' at home base. Then I gotta get back downtown."

"Savoy's place?"

Marin nodded. "After dark. I don't want to get caught in anybody's crosshairs."

He lit a cigarette and blew the smoke out the window. All of a sudden, the fatigue he had been trying to ignore dropped on him like an anchor, threatening to pull him beyond his depth into someplace dark and murky. He inhaled sharply but the nicotine had lost its taste and he flicked the cigarette into the street.

"Around eleven. Street should be clear by then."

"Spot'll still be hot," Chance said. "What you have in mind?"

"A little surveillance. Savoy probably layin' low. Tryin' to figure out what just went down. Who knows? Maybe he's holdin' a wake; that's the least he can do. A two-for-one double send-off. We park down the block and see who's bringin' condolences."

He stepped out of the car and watched Chance drive off.

The stoop was empty and the hallway was quiet. No hum of conversation. No music. He climbed the stairs, listening to the scrape of his footsteps on the marble stairs.

Margaret, Naomi, and Mama Pat looked up when he walked in. The aroma of chicken, greens, and baked bread filled the room. The table was set, and Margaret was dressed in a yellow blouse and flower-print skirt. Her hair was shining, and he saw her eyes brighten. The curve of her mouth arced into a small smile and he stared for a minute before moving around the table to kiss her.

"How you feelin'?"

"Okay. Did some cookin'. You hungry?"

Her voice came to him like the chime of a small bell, quiet and clear, with no tearful after-noise behind the sound.

He winked and was amazed when she parted her mouth so that the tips of her teeth showed. He felt a desperate fever flash within him and wanted to sink to his knees and bury his face in her lap. He wanted to hold her in his arms until she lost her breath.

Instead, he smiled at Mama Pat and Naomi and then walked to the sink to wash his hands for dinner.

The rain was coming down hard when he left the house, and Chance was waiting at the curb with the motor running. In the car, Marin looked in the back seat at the binoculars, the handcuffs, and the flashlight.

Then he looked at Chance. "Handcuffs? We goin' to a party?"

"Naw. This stuff is usually in the trunk. I got it out just in case . . ."

"In case of what? You expectin' some funny stuff?"

"I can tell you ain't never been a Boy Scout."

"They used cuffs? No wonder I wasn't in no hurry to join."

"Meanin' be prepared, man. Be prepared. No point steppin' out on a hummer. You nearly got your lights put out last night."

Marin shrugged. "I don't think that zip had my name on it. Cat was working with a pillow and he was waitin' even before I showed up. He could've pinned me when I made a dive for that gypsy but he didn't. That was a pro hit. He wasn't gettin' a bonus."

"So what's on the menu tonight?"

"A way to get to Savoy. He knows something about my baby and I'm gonna find out what it is. The longer—"

He fell silent. The rain drumming on the roof of the car sounded to him like the clatter of panicked horses. He leaned back against the seat and felt the symmetry of the Browning press into the small of his back. He had left the .38 in the cupboard and regretted now that he hadn't brought it.

But he had barely gotten the Browning out of the closet and under his shirt when Naomi had come out of the bathroom. Mama Pat was in the bedroom talking to Margaret, and he had waited for Naomi to join them but she never did.

"Take some corn bread for Chance," she had said, and cut a slice, wrapped it in waxed paper, and then searched for a small paper bag.

Marin had waited impatiently: "Listen, this is fine. It's fine. Don't need a bag. He'll probably eat it right in the car."

He had taken it quickly and headed for the door. "Back in a few hours and I'll have him drop y'all home."

He went down the stairs two at a time, thinking that when he returned, he'd have to find another, more secure place to stash the weapons.

CHAPTER 27

Day 11, 10 P.M.

A wind rose, scattering a whirl of rain-soaked litter along the sidewalk. Eighth Avenue was empty. Miss Adelaide's, open only for breakfast and lunch, was closed for the evening, and a small yellow nightlight glowed through the curtained windows. Across the avenue the Harlem Gardens, despite the rain, was gearing up and the music pounded out onto the sidewalk.

Chance maneuvered the Buick through traffic

slowed by the fog. At 125th Street, they turned east and rode through the rain-emptied thoroughfare past the Apollo, the Loew's Victoria movie theater, and Herbert's Home of Blue White Diamonds, whose glittering billboard towered over the street.

"Turn left at Lenox, go down the side street, and we can park diagonally across from the house," Marin said. "Since you got these professional peepers, we may as well use 'em."

The rain slacked off into a fine mist and Savoy's house loomed out of the fog like an abandoned hulk. Marin wiped the window and focused the lens. Chance lit a cigarette and settled behind the wheel to wait.

"Don't even see the dogs," Marin said. Then he leaned forward, steadying his elbows on the dashboard.

"Well, looka here. Company comin'. Or goin' . . ."

The woman stepped from out of the shadow of the stoop and walked quickly to the corner. She looked back once and walked faster. At the corner, she turned and disappeared into the rain. Chance turned the motor over and eased to the intersection, cruising a few yards behind. Then he pulled alongside and rolled the window down.

"Hey, pretty. What you doin' out on a night like this? Can I give you a lift?"

The girl hesitated, then stopped. "You a gypsy? I got to get downtown in a hurry."

"Well, I missed my last call," Chance said, pulling to the curb. "So I can drop you. Hop in."

Marin had removed the cuffs and put away the binoculars by the time she opened the door. When she saw him, saw that the man she had spoken to had company, she started to back away.

"Aw, no. I don't know what you got goin' on but I ain't down for no two-bit. Not tonight."

"One hundred change your mind?"

She searched the empty street, eyes flitting up and down as if she expected someone to burst around the corner. Then she appraised them quickly, her face tight with apprehension, and saw they were well dressed.

"Make it one fifty and we can talk," she whispered.

"Get in, baby. We wastin' time."

She slid into the back seat and Marin saw that she was not a woman but a young girl, still in her teens. Her eyebrows arced over wide eyes and her face held the barest trace of baby fat. Her hair was piled on her head in a two-tiered knot, and Marin was not sure if it all belonged to her. The black patent-leather raincoat was cinched firmly against a small waist, and her boots fitted against her calves. Her shoulder bag rested in her lap, and Marin was surprised at how quickly her face changed. The fear was gone. She now appeared more relaxed.

Chance drove slowly and came to a stop several blocks away. Marin recognized the area and usually tried to avoid walking through it. In daylight, it resembled a no-man's-land, torn up by design and then forgotten in the shift of political winds. Tiers of scaffolding embraced the abandoned buildings and were so old the wood had been sun-bleached white. Unsealed windows yawned open to the street, yet there was traffic on the block.

She peered through the fogged window. "Here?" she said. "You guys sure must be hungry. There's too much action. Cops nab us for sure."

Marin turned to face her. "Listen, Miss, we don't know your name but we—"

"Oh, shit! Y'all cops?" She had one hand on the door when Marin grabbed her wrist.

"Naw, naw. Nuthin' like that either. It's somethin' else. Somethin' real important."

"What is it?"

"It's about a baby, a missing baby."

She looked at him and continued to pull away. "What does that have to do with me?"

I don't know. I'm looking for some answers and thought maybe you could help."

"All right. Leggo my arm."

"You gonna run?"

"No. What you wanna know? Even if you don't want what I thought you wanted, this visit gonna cost somethin' anyway. I need the money." Her brown face paled, shadowed, paled again in the lights of passing cars. "And we gotta be quick. I gotta get downtown."

"Somebody waitin' for you?" Marin asked.

She turned to peer through the rear window. "No. Not downtown. More like uptown, if you know what I mean."

"We can get you where you got to go. First we need some talk. You just left Savoy's . . ."

The name floated in the air and her faced changed and she held up the shoulder bag flat against her midsection. Marin wondered what was in it and if they'd all end up downtown if the cops happened to roll by.

"Well, we don't want to keep you, Miss—"

"Never mind my name. What is it you want to know?"

"You ever hear Savoy or anybody in that house talk about a missing baby, a baby taken from Harlem Hospital?"

She looked at them, waiting.

"The baby's mine," Marin whispered. "My daughter's gone and I gotta find her. Someone stole her from the hospital the day after she was born. My wife's had a nervous breakdown."

She stared at him in the dim shadow of the car, sizing him up, then slowly shook her head. "Oh shit. I'm sorry. I read about that. Savoy's into too much stuff; that's why I gotta get outta here. Quick. I can't take anymore. But babies? No. They not into that. At least I ain't seen none."

Marin twisted against the front seat to face her. "The two bodyguards, Enforcer and Plug. You never heard them mention anything?"

"No, and nobody never will now. They been checked off."

"Who did 'em in?"

"Inside job, is all I can say. I don't know nuthin' else. Look, can we get rollin'?"

"Where?" Chance said, gunning the motor.

"Port Authority. I called home. Found out my auntie ain't doin' too good. She's the only one left and I need to tell her, tell her that I . . ."

Her voice drifted off, and Marin listened in the silence to the hum of the motor as Chance pulled away from the curb.

"How long you been here?" Marin said.

She looked up and shrugged. "In the city or in that house?"

"Both . . ."

"Six months in the city and too long in that house."

"You ain't but sixteen, I bet," Chance said to the rearview mirror. "How come you—how you get in this—situation so fast?"

"One of those things, I guess."

She had lit a cigarette and settled back in the seat. She unfastened her coat and crossed her legs but kept the shoulder bag balanced in her lap. "I come up from Virginia. My mama had died and I came here lookin' for my daddy. Two months after I found 'im, his heart took him out. His new wife, my stepmomma, was probably scared I was gonna cut into a little bit of that insurance money and she didn't want me around.

"Told her that wasn't the case but we had words, more and more every day, and finally I had to go. I mean she put me out without a dime. I got caught stealin' a muffin and the judge sent me to Spofford. Sneaked out of there and wound up at Port Authority thinkin' maybe I could hide out on a bus some way and head back home. At least my aunt or somebody who know me would give me a hand till I could get back on my feet.

"But I got picked up by this cop. Flashed his badge and talked heavy shit about sendin' me to a woman's prison because I looked old enough to be in one. Talked about what some of them was gonna do to me there."

"This cop. What did he look like?" Marin said.

"White. Stringy blond hair."

"Know his name?"

"After all this time, I sure do. It's Leahy."

Marin turned away to stare out of the window. He reached in his pocket and his hands shook. He lit a cigarette and listened as the sound of her seemed to fill the interior of the auto.

"That night he drove me around for a long time, just talkin'. Said if I behaved right, he'd forget everything, wouldn't take me in. He had a friend could put me up for the night and next day, he'd see about gettin' me a job or somethin'. A chance to make some money 'cause he liked me, liked the way I looked and all. Said I could make enough to get my own pad, phone, nice rags, and all. And he'd look out for me.

"He talked nice and slow and quiet. I went with him and he introduced me to Savoy . . ."

She stopped talking, and neither Marin nor Chance thought she would say anything more. She was out of there, on her way to a bus that would take her back home.

They were moving through traffic along Central Park West and the blocks passed in slow succession. Marin glanced at the few people still out in the rain: dog walkers, deliverymen with their grocery carts, shoppers weighed down with bags and stepping out of cabs. He looked up at the lighted windows of elegant apartments as she spoke again.

"It was like three nights outside and four days inside."

"That some kinda schedule?" Chance said, looking in the mirror.

"It's a schedule, all right. A real tight tough one. There's a factory in there, and I don't care about talkin' 'cause I'm on my way. Gonna dime 'em out soon as I get where I'm goin'."

She rested her bag on the seat now and leaned forward. "Those few months was enough for me. Three nights on the stroll and four standin' at the table. He got different rooms for different clients, you know. But the factory on the top floor is the main thing. There's a drain under the table. Big like a sewer drain. Flush the stuff in an emergency but emergency ain't gonna happen 'cause he payin' big time. He got four girls. I was one of 'em. They young. Sixteen, seventeen, and fifteen. Scared of him but more scared to leave. He know their whole families. When I get where I'm goin', I'm a be far enough away to drop a dime he can't trace. Even Leahy don't know. Told 'im I was from Nevada. Anyway, I'm gonna blow the blanket off so the rest of the girls can get the hell out too.

"So, the deal is two of us stand at the table. We cut, weigh, and bag. We don't sit down and don't wear no clothes. We naked except for a plastic shower cap on our hair and a cotton mask over our nose and mouth.

"Now the thing is, there's a shower in this little bathroom off the main room which we ain't allowed to use till we finish. There's no door, no shower curtains, and the wall is a two-way mirror. Savoy tells us that so we don't make no mistake about hidin' product.

"The thing about this shower is we couldn't take one until Leahy get through with us. Called us his flavor of the day. When our shift is up, we go into another room and he there waitin', naked. No sooner we walk in when he down on his knees, tongue out, lickin' what he call residue off us. He was like a dog ain't had water for a week. Instead of takin' the stuff up the nose or in the arm like Savoy's other people, Leahy sprinkled it on us and licked it off. We had names. Chocolate Power, Vanilla Crème, Mocha. Strange shit like that."

"What did Savoy do?" Marin asked.

"Savoy, he sit there with a glass of Dom Pee in his hand, no clothes on, and he watch and sip. Sometimes Leahy get so carried away, he forget he got a tongue and he start usin' his teeth. Bite Vanilla so hard one time, she had to slap him to make him turn her loose.

"He was ready now, with all that stuff cookin' up his brain, to strangle her. But Savoy raised his hand and Enforcer stepped up and toned him down."

The girl lit another cigarette. In the brief silence, Marin thought of the makeshift bars and the mama-san houses half a world away that had sprung up like mushrooms near the base where the soldiers congregated on payday. The lines were longest and the fights more violent outside the houses where the girls were the youngest.

"Like I said," the girl continued. "Savoy was strange. All he did was watch and grin. Enforcer didn't like girls so he just stand there, bug-eyed like he was diggin' a freak show and couldn't get enough. Leahy would do such a good job, front to back, top to bottom, there wasn't no need for a shower—except you had to, just had to grab that soap and scrub your skin till it start to hurt."

"Nobody—none of the girls said anything?" Chance asked.

She looked at him and shook her head. "What was there to say? They was scared. They got family. So all that money they was pullin' in went to payin' high-rise rents, supportin' relatives, buyin' cars, clothes. That's what they settled for because underneath it all, they was scared. They open their mouth, they get contracted."

"What about Plug. What did he do?"

"His job was to drop by the different houses at different times, pay a visit to wherever they lived every now and then. He was a reminder that kept every lip locked. I don't have no family here so it was easier for me to break out. I had to get out. I think my auntie is dyin'."

She glanced out of the window and was silent. When she spoke again, her voice seemed too large and too loud for the small space.

"We was high-priced hostages," she said. "Work the tables some days, work his special customers the other times. Leahy got everything free 'cause they're partners."

"Enforcer and Plug. How'd they get knocked off?" Marin said.

"I don't know and I don't care."

The answer had come so quickly they both knew she was lying.

Marin wanted to ask about "the inside job" she had mentioned earlier but changed his mind.

At 42nd Street and Ninth Avenue, she settled for one hundred dollars and stayed in the car until Marin returned with the ticket.

"Bus leaves at one-twenty. Gate 17. I'll walk behind you in case you run into any static."

At one-thirty the ride back uptown was quiet until Chance said. "What's on your mind?"

"Nuthin'."

"Come on. It's all on your face. After hearin' all that shit, you must be thinkin' somethin'."

"You right. I am thinkin' about somethin'. I'm packin' and if I see that ice-cream motherfucka, I'm gonna take him off."

"He's a cop, Marin. No can do. You'd have the whole city on you like white-on-rice."

"I don't give a shit," he whispered.

Marin leaned back against the seat and squeezed his eyes shut, the focus of his anger and frustration shifting. "Savoy's not in the game. He doesn't have Meredith so I'm right back at square one. But I'm gonna find her if I have to go block by block, offer a reward with dollars I don't have. I'm gonna turn over every stone."

The car moved along the West Side Highway. The fog lifted from the river and fragments of light blinked through the infrequent breaches of the Jersey Palisades. A small boat maneuvered through the water, heading toward the lights of the George Washington Bridge. Its horn sounded small in the distance. Chance glanced at Marin. His eyes were open again, wide and unfocused.

CHAPTER 28

Day 12, 2 A.M.

Chance turned off the highway at 125th Street and drove downtown. At 118th Street, he pulled up at the Cecil Hotel. The sign above Minton's Playhouse glimmered in the dark and the entrance to the club was crowded.

"A taste'll get your head together. Then you think about what you want to do."

"I meant what I said about Leahy. That's what I want to do."

Chance rested his elbows on the steering wheel and rubbed his eyes with his balled fists. "Listen, man, your kid is still out there and you worryin' about a snot ball. Forget him. You gotta concentrate. The longer it takes to track your kid, the colder the trail gets. After a while, she'll only be a memory if you don't do somethin' soon. You tie your brain up over that motherfucka, you slide away from your mission."

A soft silence peculiar to the night lay over the short block despite the hum of the crowd at the club's entrance. Marin glanced at them, then gazed straight ahead. "That's what I'm tryin' to tell you, Chance. I haven't mentioned this to Margaret but some stuff is hard to keep to yourself."

"Like what?"

"I keep thinkin' it's possible we may never see Meredith again."

"Come on Marin, you—"

"I mean, suppose she grow up with whoever snatched her, grows up to be tall and beautiful, just like Margaret. And suppose she finally run away to wander the streets looking for us, her real folks. And while she's lookin', falls into the hands of somebody like Leahy."

Chance looked away. "Man, your mind is gettin' too far ahead of things. That ain't likely to happen."

"Maybe not. Then maybe it could. Look at what we just left. That girl wasn't lyin'. She's lucky to get outta there. That Leahy is like a dog without a leash. Motherfucka has got to go."

They sat in silence until Marin sighed. "No way I'm gettin' any shut-eye tonight."

They left the car and walked into the club. Inside it was dark, the air heavy with smoke, music, and conversation. The tables were full so they joined the standees at the bar.

The spotlight dimmed and the piano player slowly escorted Al Hibbler off stage, seated him at a small table, then returned to the piano.

Marin ordered a drink and checked his watch. Not quite 3 A.M. The

52nd Street spots were still busy and most of the players wouldn't be heading uptown before four. Once they stepped in, they'd jam through what was left of the night, break, and start again at the time most other folks were hitting the streets to make it to their day jobs.

He scanned the bar and knew that half of those bending elbows would probably be rushing home at seven to shower away the residue of cigarette smoke and whatever they had been sipping, then step out again to stand up all the way downtown on the A, standing up even if the seat in front of them was vacant. No sitting and nodding past their stop. Too many guys had blown too many jobs that way.

A short man in a porkpie hat, striped shirt, and black pants with red suspenders climbed up to the stage. He held a drink in one hand and a cigarette in the other and leaned into the mike to announce the next number.

"And now let's welcome . . ."

The name was lost in the noise of the crowd as the young woman stepped onto the stage. She was tall and thin and her Afro framed her face like a velvet cloud. The spotlight shifted from the man in the porkpie to the piano man, who riffled through an intro. Then the light shone on the young woman. She opened her mouth and the notes moved through the crowd, quieting them with a throaty wine-sap sweetness.

Marin listened, nodding his head. He had been standing in this very spot years earlier, and the voice now floating toward him washed time and distance away.

He remembered the door opening and a hum of excitement surging through the room like a breaker. The spotlight splashing on blinding white and Dinah Washington, in a strapless black-sequined gown and pale mink stole, escorted by three men, pushing through the crowd like a hot cur-rent. The bartender had raised his hand and a table was quickly set up front and center. One of her escorts held a chair out but instead of sitting, Dinah had dropped the stole on the table, kicked off her shoes, and climbed onto the stage. The spotlight had softened, then narrowed to envelop her face in a small yellow halo.

She had closed her eyes and opened her mouth, and the clear, cool sound of "Drown in My Own Tears" rolled through the crowd. Talk died at the bar. The clink of glass was put on hold. Murmurs of recognition, appreciation faded.

She had held her hand up and out, silencing the musicians, then clasped her arms to sing into a deep, reverential silence.

Marin stood with his mouth open. He had heard her once before, onstage in the large, crowded Apollo, but that night she sang just a few feet away, close enough to for him to see the lines of concentration and the history of pain around her closed eyes.

The young woman onstage sounded almost like Dinah, and Marin listened, his thoughts and feelings riding every note. Her voice conjured up memory that was strangling him, dreams that had turned to nightmares from which he could not waken. His throat tightened with a feeling that was rising out of control and he turned to the bar and emptied his glass in one swallow.

"I gotta get outta here," he whispered.

On their way to the door, Marin would have walked right past Benjamin had he not tapped him on the shoulder.

"Well, I'll be damn . . . What's—"

"Outside in a minute," Benjamin said. He did not look at either of them but kept his eyes fixed on the spotlight. Marin glanced beyond him, following his gaze, but could make out nothing past the young woman's closed eyes and the play of the light against her red gown.

Outside, Marin and Chance walked the few steps to the corner and waited. The rain clouds had blown away and the sky was a flat blackboard pierced by faint pins of light.

"That's that cop, ain't it," Chance said. "What the hell was that all about?"

"Don't know yet."

"You gonna mention Savoy?"

Marin shook his head. "I mention Savoy, I gotta mention Leahy, and I don't know which side of the fence this guy is leanin' on. I ain't settin' myself up to get it in the neck. From the way the girl talked, Savoy got a big money operation goin' on and he spreadin' lotta dollars to make sure it stays that way. Unh, unh. Let Benjamin do—"

"So what's goin' on?" Benjamin said.

He seemed to appear out of the night. His tan linen jacket hung limply on his shoulders and his frame did not appear as large as it once had.

"How's your wife doin'?" he said.

"Little better . . . I left a few messages for you. No callback. What's happenin'?"

The short street between Eighth and St. Nicholas Avenues was filled now with cars pulling up to the club.

Benjamin looked across the street where four men piled out of a cab. Each carried an instrument. A second cab pulled up and a bass player struggled to ease his bass out. The jam was about to start. Benjamin leaned from one foot to the other and looked at Marin in the dim light.

"You didn't hear from me because I'm in the street."

"You suspended. Damn. What happened?"

"Stepped on some toes is all I can say. Be out for three more weeks."

"That's a long stretch . . ."

"Damn long." He turned to go, then hesitated. "If you come up with anything, zip the local and contact the D.A. I believe your baby's right here in Harlem, Taylor. I have no tips, no clues. Nothing like that. And I know what I'm saying sounds kind of unscientific but I'm in the street and there's no restrictions in the street. So that's what I'm feeling. Sometimes you gotta listen to your feelings."

He nodded and walked back toward the club. Two more cabs pulled to the curb. The passengers stepped out. They were tourists, filled with noisy expectation and the peculiar excitement brought on by night in foreign territory. Benjamin walked past them and made his way back inside.

The cabs pulled away, the club door slammed, pinching off the music, and Marin and Chance were alone, standing in the quiet of the block.

They walked to the car and Chance looked up as he unlocked the door. Marin was staring at the lights over the entrance through which Benjamin had disappeared. He rested his elbow on the roof of the car and leaned over holding his side as if he had just finished the last lap of a losing race.

"I got a call one night before all this other shit happened," he whispered, gazing at the blinking sign. "I had been outside Savoy's pad and as soon as I stepped back home, the phone rang. Somebody asked what the fuck I was doin'. Said somethin' was goin' on and it didn't concern me. It was Benjamin. He was mad as hell then. Now I recognize the voice."

CHAPTER 29

Day 12, 7 A.M.

Marin dreamed the phone was ringing and turned over. The ringing did not stop, and he sat up, moved quickly to the kitchen, and lifted the receiver. The cat clock with the wagging tail and roving eyes read 7 A.M.

He had gotten three hours of sleep. His eyes burned and his neck ached as he leaned against the wall.

"Yeah?"

"I called last night. You get my message?"

"Who's this?"

"Jimmy."

"What's happenin'?"

"Somethin' I forgot to mention the other night." Jimmy dropped his voice and Marin strained to hear him. "So much talk move over that bar, I forget sometimes. But Plug and his pal had also talked about a barber somewhere on 120th Street. But with all the news about them gettin' blown away, one right behind the other, I forgot to mention this to you. Anyway, the barber's name is Paulie. Check him out. See what's happenin'. Seems a woman was in there gettin' her hair did and was cryin' about the guy they were lookin' for. Said she had red hair."

"Thanks, man. Thanks. Talk to you later. Let you know what's happenin'."

He hung up and turned around to see Margaret standing at the bedroom door. He wondered how long she had been there and how much she had heard.

She moved toward him with her hand outstretched, then stopped.

"You were so late gettin' in last night, I thought something had happened to you. I thought—"

"No. No. Just checkin' some leads. That was Jimmy, the bartender at the Fat Man. Wanted to know if we was all right."

She studied him in the half light. "Oh, yes. He called last night. Mama left a note on the refrigerator for you to call him back. Now he's callin' again. And so early? It's not even eight o'clock."

"I know. He hasn't seen me in a while and thought he'd catch me at home. He's just comin' in from an all-nighter and wanted to check before he hit the sack. Everything's all right. Said to tell you hello."

She turned toward the bedroom but not before he caught the expression on her face. He knew she did not believe him. He followed and sat beside her. She put her head on his shoulder and closed her eyes. "Everyone's talking around me and no one's saying anything.

The few times they open their mouths, I see right through them. Don't you lie to me too, Marin. I don't want this, don't need this from you."

"You're right. You're right." He could feel the catch in her breath and wondered if she was about to cry.

"I am going to find Meredith. I promise you, baby. That's what I'm going to do."

She did not answer but lay back down and rolled away, leaving him alone on the edge of the bed.

"Baby? You all right?"

"I'm all right. Yes."

"I'll make us some coffee and we'll talk. I got a few ideas I want you to listen to."

She did not answer, and he rose and went into the kitchen. The battered aluminum coffeepot was on the stove and he filled it with coffee and water and lit the jet under it, wondering what he was going to say. He was going downtown to see a barber named Paulie but beyond that, what more could he tell her?

He watched the coffee pump through the stem and hit the glass top and thought of the young girl who had gotten away. He thought of Enforcer. Gone. And how Leahy probably had set it up to have Plug taken out. He was sure of it. A neat, public, official execution. Plug had reached for his piece and gotten it in the chest. Both were gone and took whatever information they had with them.

The coffee aroma spread through the kitchen. He turned the jet off, set up a tray, and carried two cups to the bedroom.

The barbershop on Eighth Avenue near 120th Street was a long narrow space with a wide front window filled with large aloe plants. It was crowded although it was not yet 11 A.M. James Brown was wailing his personal anthem through two large speakers positioned near the door. "Say it loud! I'm black and I'm proud!"

Marin took a seat near the rear and read the nameplates over the four chairs. Paulie, from the sign in the window, was the owner. He was tall, with broad shoulders and a face that seemed chiseled from ebony. A red, black, and green bandana controlled his blown-out curly Afro. His chair was near the window, and he gestured toward Marin with his scissors. "You waitin' for me, you number four, okay?"

"No problem. I'll be by the door. Takin' a smoke."

Outside, the awning offered a sliver of shade and little else. The heat penetrated its striped fabric as Marin patted his pocket for a cigarette and came up empty.

. . . Step to that corner store. I'm number four, he won't get to me for a while. Later, I run by Carver for some coin. Not much left in the kitty.

When he returned from the store, Paulie was standing outside with a young woman. Marin leaned against a parked car, lit a cigarette, and pretended to ignore the argument. The woman waved her arms as Paulie tried to talk. Her hair was clipped short enough for her scalp to show and the little that remained was dyed a bright tangerine that seemed to sparkle in the sun. Marin studied her brown face and decided that even with the strange-color hair, and with her face folded in a deep frown, she was a pretty woman.

"Listen Paulie. You're my cousin and got nothing to say?"

"I'm sayin' you ain't gettin' your hands on my weapon, Thelma. They trace it to me, my barber's license go up in smoke. I ain't supposed to be holdin' no piece anyway. You knock your man, I vacation upstate, who's gonna feed my kids?"

"He ain't my man . . ."

"Not no more he ain't. How you let somebody like him into your life anyway? I always said you coulda done a lot better than that. He was a loser, way past zero. But no. You was always needin' to rescue, redeem, rehabilitate. Shit like that. You shoulda stuck to stray animals. You feed 'em, they respect you 'cause they know where they next square is comin' from. A snake woulda treated you better."

"Paulie, listen. He took Mama's bracelets. Your aunt's bracelets. I don't have any kids and those same pieces that was gonna go to your daughter when I close my eyes, they're gone. He got all ten of 'em plus my African necklaces. I gotta get 'em back. I'm not gonna kill nobody, just scare him enough to get back what's mine."

"Girl, I know you. When you see that man's face, you gonna want to put your foot in it. You are not gettin' my piece. Besides, you was cryin' that he skipped to parts unknown. Where you gonna start to look?"

The woman shook her head and her earrings shimmered in the sun. "Right here. He ain't got brains enough to go but so far. Take it block by block if I have to. Go to West Hell if I have to. But I'm gettin' my stuff, you can bet your bottom buck on it. If his heart happen to stop while I'm at it, then that's just tough shit."

Paulie looked up and down Eighth Avenue, drew a breath, then raised his hand. "Thelma, listen. You knew the man was bad news. You knew it from when he pulled that first fade. You ain't learned nothin'? Nobody's dick is that good. Nobody's."

"It ain't about that no more. He was so banged up, he couldn't do that much anyway. I want those bracelets and I'm gonna get 'em. You watch and see."

"Suit yourself. Just don't come to me for no bail."

"Paulie!"

"I got to get to work. I'm backed up, baby. But don't you go runnin' off on the wild side. I be talkin' to you later."

The door closed and she stood there, undecided whether to follow her cousin inside. She sighed and turned away, caught Marin's glance, and stared at him narrowly. Her hair and earrings glinted in the sun. "You enjoyin' the show?"

Her eyes were on fire and Marin decided to answer her directly. "Didn't mean any harm but from what I heard, maybe you and I are lookin' for the same guy."

She glanced at the barbershop. Paulie was talking on the phone and had his back to the window. She could see his hand in the air as

he spoke. The music was still loud and she faced Marin again, squinting as she sized him up.

"You look familiar. Do I know you?"

"Not directly. Name's Marin Taylor. That ring a bell?"

"No."

"But you might know something else. Feel like walking?"

Before they reached Morningside Avenue and took a seat on a
bench facing the park, Marin knew that the man, Conroy Henderson,
who had stabbed him on the viaduct and the man who had run out on
Thelma were one and the same.

"He was always doin' somethin' dirty," Thelma said. "But somebody caught up with him. When I picked him up this second time, he
had been beat so bad he couldn't even stand up. Had to drag his
snivelin' butt up three flights of stairs and lay him on the rug. That's
how bad he was.

"Cleaned him up, bought new clothes, fed him special food to get
his strength back. All that. Now I expected him to leave, because we
had talked on it—you know how it is when things ain't workin' out.
Well, he walked but not before he helped himself to my jewelry. The
man has no conscience. Just like his brother who took that dive. He's
a thug and would backstab his own mama if he have to."

Marin shook his head, remembering how Conroy and his brother
had come up on him that night out of nowhere.

"I need to find out if he had any connection to my daughter's disappearance," Marin said. "Two guys were overheard talking about
him, how he might know where she is."

"The baby that was taken from Harlem about two weeks ago? I
read about that. I'm sorry. I'm really sorry . . ." She paused, then said,
"How come you aren't after those two guys, find out what they
know?"

"I wasn't fast enough," Marin said. "They both got taken out."

Thelma sat with her hands on her knees, watching a scatter of pigeons at the curb peck at a piece of bread. Their cawing was loud and

nervous and they began to peck at each other. A car backfired, causing them to take to the air. They flew out of sight before Thelma spoke again.

"I don't know if he knows anything but I damn sure will help you find him. And the sooner the better, before he unloads my stuff. I can't replace my mama's bracelets. I just can't."

"Here's my number," Marin said. "And here's the number of a friend of mine if you can't reach me. His name's Chance."

Thelma inspected the piece of paper and turned to him. She smiled and her face lost the line of frowns.

"Chance. That's an interesting name. What's he like?"

"Kinda tall, brown, close-cut hair, nice dresser, drives a big beat-up Buick and thinkin' of gettin' a new one—"

"He married?"

"No."

"Divorced?"

"No."

"Kids?"

"Not that I know of."

Her smile broadened at each reply. "How long have you known him?"

"Long enough. We Aye Bee Cees. Ran into him in 'Nam. Found he was a home boy, and we been tight ever since."

She examined the phone number on the slip as if to conjure a picture of Chance. Then she nodded and tucked the paper in her pocket. "I'll call. Either you or him. We gonna find Conroy. Harlem ain't but so big. You'll hear from me sooner than you think."

CHAPTER 30

Day 15, 3 P.M.

Ask any of the old-timers and they will tell you that the real Harlem extends from the northern edge of Central Park at 110th Street to the viaduct at 155th Street where the old Polo Grounds once housed the New York Giants.

At 145th Street, it takes less than a half hour to walk from river to river. From the Harlem River at Lenox Avenue to the Hudson on Riverside Drive. They say it's a small community geographically, and gets even smaller when a message, set adrift to float on the prevailing current, finds its mark.

Like a note taped to the leg of a homing pigeon, word got to Conroy that someone needed to pick up a last-minute present. An anniversary celebration, they said.

He took time out from his search for Sadie and sauntered into the barbershop with a small plastic-wrapped package tucked under his arm. He pulled Paulie aside.

"Heard somebody lookin' for some quality," he said. Not too softly just in case Paulie wasn't interested and someone else in the place might be.

Paulie looked him up and down before he answered.

"Yeah. Have a seat in the back. Be with you in a minute."

Then he turned to the man in his chair, brushed his neck with the soft whisk, removed the towel, and held up the mirror. The man nodded, paid, and left the shop, and Paulie waited until the door closed before he walked down the narrow aisle. He sat down in the chair opposite Conroy and blew out a breath. "Sometimes it's hard on the feet, you know. Standin' all day. But what the hell. It's a livin', man. Best I can do. . . ."

The second chair near the window was still occupied but the barber cutting the customer's hair had his back to them. The music masked the conversation in the otherwise empty shop but Conroy glanced over his shoulder before he unwrapped the package. He removed the tissue and Paulie leaned forward and rested his chin in his hand. A minute was all he needed to recognize the familiar objects.

"These are kinda nice," he said, picking one up to examine. He kept his voice even. "Me and my lady been married nearly ten years through thick shit and thin. Got three kids. Need to do something real good for her. You got anything else?"

"Yeah. Some necklaces. They African stuff. The real authentic deal. Got 'em from an importer. Since you like these bracelets, I'll let you have the necklaces too for a good price."

"How much we talkin' about?"

Conroy sat back and pursed his lips. "Lessee. Package deal. Eighteen K bangles plus the—"

"You sure the necklaces is African?"

"Sure as I'm sittin' here. Bought 'em from a guy whose pop is a famous African prince. Forgot what tribe, but he so authentic, he got marks on his face. You don't see too much of that up here so I can testify for the stuff. They for real."

Paulie nodded, wanting to ask Conroy about the web of scars on his own face. They also looked authentic, fresh from his last heist. He wanted to slide from his chair, with his hand wrapped around his straight razor, and put his knee in Conroy's chest and carve a few more insignias on his grinning face. But the call had been made and the play was in motion. He made an effort to be patient.

"So okay," he said. "How much you askin'?"

"Lessee. A gee."

Paulie looked away. "A thousand is kinda steep."

"Okay. I see you a hard-workin' brother and I respect that. And you got other bills. I know how that is. Three kids must keep you in trouble, moneywise, sooo . . . how about nine hundred?"

As he spoke he spread the bangles out on a towel on the counter where the reflection in the mirror highlighted the etched gold.

"Eight and a half and you got a deal," Paulie said.

Conroy scratched his chin and Paulie waited, thinking of his cousin and how the hell she could have hooked up with such a damn dumb, dim-witted motherfucka.

"Eight-fifty? Man you stickin' me up in broad daylight."

"It's seven o'clock." Paulie smiled. "When can I see the necklaces?"

"I get 'em here in five minutes, if you want . . ."

Paulie held up his hand and looked around. "No. Wait till around nine. I close up then, and I don't want no eyes peepin' my stash. Folks got no respect for other people's hard-earned stuff, you know what I mean?"

"I hear you, brother. I know how it is."

"So, you be here at nine and everything be all right."

Paulie walked with him to the door and watched as he disappeared around the corner. Then he reached for the phone again. He dialed, listened for a second, nodding his head as if the speaker was in the room. Then he answered, "Nine o'clock. That's cool. Shadow him a block or so, then dust 'im off real nice. He'll be carryin' $850. I want to see $750, okay?"

He hung up and picked up the wide-angled broom. The other barber had finished and was cleaning his instruments. Paulie swept around and in between the chairs. The sun had set and dark shadows stretched across the sidewalk like elongated fingers. Paulie leaned on the broom and looked through the plate glass at the old-fashioned barber's candy-striped pole. The place had been his father's, and Paulie had swept the hair and dust off the floor since he was nine years old. He learned the trade and took over when the old man died. The pole still worked and he watched the red-and-white stripe whir in a diagonal up and down.

. . . I got to pull Thelma's coat. Thought she had bad taste but damn, this cat ain't no taste at all. Raggedy togs, broke down sneakers, head ain't seen a comb since Hector.

He put the broom away and made a mental note to tap Thelma for the one hundred dollars when he returned her jewelry.

CHAPTER 31

Day 15, 10 P.M.

"*W*ho jumped you, Conroy? Who did this?"

His mother wrung her hands as he stumbled down the hallway, tripping over boxes and bags in the dark.

When he didn't answer, she cried, "It was Savoy, wasn't it. I told you he didn't forget. He sent his boys and he'll send 'em again until you pay up."

Conroy eased down onto the dilapidated chair. He hurt all over and wondered if his arm was broken. He did not speak but his mind was racing.

. . . Savoy. Motherfucka didn't waste no time. Got new muscle on the job already. Musta been pinnin' me for a while. Like it was all planned. They didn't even say nuthin'. Just stepped out of nowhere and got down to business.

He heard his mother move down the hall with a basin of water, saw her balance it on a rack over a can of sterno. When it warmed, she brought it to him and placed it along with a sponge on the plastic milk crate. "I poured some witch hazel in it also. That'll take some of the ache away. Meanwhile, you better figure out what you gonna do. I don't have no money to bury anybody."

She disappeared down the hall and left Conroy alone in the dark. He tried to close his eyes but his head was spinning.

The two men had stepped out like pros. One had cut off his breath in a quick chokehold while the other went in his pockets, cleaning him out in less time than it took to blink. Then, without a word to him or to each other, they punched the air out of him until he collapsed to his knees. He curled to the ground and the rain of kicks came hard and steady as boulders in a landslide.

An hour later, when he had managed to open his eyes, Eighth Avenue was deserted except for a stray dog nosing through bags of garbage near the edge of the alley. A bus empty of passengers rumbled past, braked, but did not stop. A few doors away, party sounds spilled faintly through a second-story window. It mixed with the ringing in his ears as he pulled himself from the pavement.

He held to the walls of buildings, felt his way around lampposts until, hand over hand, he made his way back to his mother's house.

He squeezed the water from the sponge and pressed it tight against his head.

Next time'll probably be my last. Savoy don't play. I got to find that kid. The money I get is the only thing gonna save my ass.

He sat in the dark, thinking of Sadie, knowing that by this time she had no intention of giving up the baby without a fight. That's why she had left Atlanta without telling him, went into hiding when she returned to Harlem. She was here somewhere, he was sure of it. He could feel her presence.

His nose was still bleeding so he leaned back against the chair, staring at the arc of lights racing across the ceiling from the passing cars. When the lights faded, the shadows closed in deeper and darker.

He made up his mind.

. . . It's her or me. My clock's tickin'. Shit, if it wasn't for her, I'd be on easy street already. Take her off. Ain't no big thing.

Two nights later, later than he had planned, he lounged on a stoop across the street near Sadie's old building and watched the movement of people. A group of teenagers leaned against the low iron railing near the entrance and he listened to their loud talk.

. . . Could ask one of them if they seen her, or somebody look like her.

The boom box was blasting and their laughter was even louder when they left the railing and formed a circle on the sidewalk. The circle enlarged as passersby paused to listen. The boys, small and agile, sounded like the Jackson Five. Conroy moved across the street and loitered at the edge of the onlookers, wondering which one of the teenagers looked easy enough to approach. The boy in the lead was bowing to noisy applause.

"Who can do better?" another boy called, assuming the role of master of cermeony. He was about eleven, short and slightly overweight. His midsection spilled over the elasticized band of his Bermuda shorts and his T-shirt stretched across his chest. He called again. "Who top this? Nobody. So come on. Let's show some love." He took off his cap and moved among the onlookers. "Anything that jingle be much appreciated," he said. "This ain't no exercise. This is talent. You don't know it, but you lookin' at the Sweet Soul Serenaders."

A few dimes and quarters fell into the cap but the core of the crowd thinned out, shifting away from the proposition. The boy approached Conroy, extending his cap. "Whatcha say, mister?"

Conroy fumbled in his pocket and came up with a quarter. Before he dropped the coin into the cap, he asked, "You live in that building?"

"Which one?"

"The one right behind you?"

"Why?" The boy looked at him narrowly and withdrew the cap. "We makin' too much noise or somethin? You sure don't look like no cop. What's up?"

"Nuthin'. I'm tryin' to find a lady live on the block. My sister. She got a kid and I heard the kid was sick. We ain't spoke in a few months. Somebody called me but didn't leave no address. Just said it was this block. I need to see her."

The boy waited for Conroy to drop the quarter. When he hesitated, he shook his head and looked away. Two girls now were dancing in line behind the singers. They were humming and showcasing their backup moves. The crowd had reformed, clapping, more enthusiastic. It was time to get back to work. The boy nodded again and shrugged, knowing that the quarter wasn't going into the cap and he was wasting time. "Ain't seen nuthin', mister."

He walked away and Conroy slipped the coin back in his pocket. He walked away also. Then it occurred to him that few people would have seen her. Instead of going to the park or lounging in front of the building, Sadie usually took the baby up to the roof.

. . . Said the air was cleaner and she could see stuff farther away, whatever that was supposed to mean. What the fuck was she lookin' for? The damn dollars was right there layin' in her lap. All she had to do was look down.

Tomorrow, if the weather's right, I'll go roof hoppin' . . .

It rained the next day but he went out anyway, hiding beneath a broken umbrella his mother had scavenged from somewhere. When anyone passed, he dipped the umbrella and averted his gaze.

The stoop was empty when he entered the block. He walked past the house and paused in front of the adjoining building, then glanced behind him.

Rain beat against the parked cars and the tops of the garbage cans. He strode into the lobby and climbed the stairs to the roof, listening to the wet squish of his worn sneakers in the empty hallway. The door to the roof swung back on rusted hinges, as if it had not been opened in a long time. He steadied the umbrella and climbed over the low concrete barrier between the buildings. The clotheslines were empty. He walked, bent over against the rain, to the spot where Sadie usually sat and found what he was looking for.

The small pink baby rattle floated in a puddle clogged with candy wrappers and lipstick-stained cigarette butts. He picked up the rattle and continued to search. A few steps away, he found a hair brush.

. . . This is hers. I seen her with it. Said it was old. Ain't but so many with a tortoise-shell trim. She musta been up here, daydreamin' in the dark as usual, and forgot and left it.

He examined it in the downpour, then slipped the brush and the rattle in his pocket and retraced his steps.

CHAPTER 32

Day 19, 4 P.M.

Conroy's mother sat in a chair, watching as he bandaged his arm and fitted it into a sling. He had a bandage around his forehead just visible below the rim of his straw hat.

"You hurt that bad, why you goin' out?"

"Got somethin' to do."

"Seems to me, you oughtta lay low till you feel up to goin' out. Bright sunshine outside. No tellin' who you might run into. This is broad daylight. You takin' a chance."

Conroy peered in the broken mirror and shook his head, satisfied at the image. He knew he was taking a chance, but this one was a sure thing.

Last night, he had sat by the window, listening to the rain drum against the glass. It had eased off at dawn and stopped altogether an hour later. By the time the sun came out, he had discarded several game plans before settling on one he knew would work.

"Stop naggin'. Somebody's holdin' somethin' for me and I got to pick it up." He did not wave but stepped out the door and did not look back.

 On Lenox Avenue, he moved cautiously, with the brim of his straw hat slanted over his face and his sunglasses far down on his nose. The distance between his mother's place and Sadie's was less than ten blocks, but the avenue was crowded and noisy with vendors, children skating, folks taking in the sun in front of narrow doorways, waiting to hear if they'd had any luck with the last number.

A few glanced at his bandaged arm, and one old woman lounging in a lawn chair sucked her teeth and nudged her neighbor. "There go another junkie busted another vein. He ain't learned; serve his stupid butt right."

Said it loud enough for him to hear. His stare turned into a scowl.

. . . *Fuck yourself left, right, and sideways, bitch,* was what he wanted to say but there were too many people in the street for him to do anything but mouth the words under his breath. He moved on, cursing to himself because he could not confront her the way he wanted to.

Several blocks away, he calmed enough to focus once more on his plan for Sadie.

. . . *Go at it nice and easy. Lay the story on light so she don't run. She can look after the kid till that money note is in the daddy's hand. When the cash comes, I give her up. Cops do what they want with her. I'll settle with Savoy and be in the wind before they blink.*

Sadie's block was also busy and he hesitated on the corner. An iceman had a crowd around him, music blasted from a parked car, and a street sweeper rolled by slowly, adding to the noise and confusion. He walked near the sweeper midway into the block, then hurried across the street and climbed the steps into the building adjacent to Sadie's. The dim hallway was silent except for faint strands of music, which faded as he made his way to the roof landing.

He eased the door open slowly to minimize the scrape of the rusted hinges. It made a creaking noise anyway. He stepped across the low barrier onto the next roof and saw her sitting with the baby in her lap. She turned her head expectantly at the sound, then froze, her face blank with surprise. The baby squirmed in her arms and she pressed the child to her.

Conroy took off his hat so that the bandage showed. His walk slowed to a limp.

"Sadie," he murmured. He held his bandaged arm stiffly in front of him. "Baby."

He eased down next to her on a small crate and squeezed his eyes shut for a second, then opened them to glance at the baby. The child had grown in three weeks. It had been almost three weeks. He wondered how much interest he now owed Savoy.

He looked up. Sadie had risen from her seat and was staring at him with her mouth open, and he knew he had to talk. Come at her swift and sweet before she had time to get herself together.

"Baby," he murmured. "I been lookin' everywhere for you. I was real worried. I even went back to the baby's father, thinkin' he might know somethin'. But he didn't believe me. See what he did? Nearly killed me. Put me in the hospital. I just got out and started lookin' for you again. I told him I didn't know where you was. But he said you was stashed somewhere and I knew where you were. I didn't know nuthin' and it was drivin' me crazy. I'm glad you in one piece. I didn't know what had happened to you, baby."

She had backed away from him. When she found her voice, the words came at him like small stones. "Conroy, you ain't gettin' Babygirl. She's mine. Nobody ain't gettin' her, you hear me."

He sat there, surprised by the emotion in her voice, and surprised that she had named the baby. As if it was really hers. He glanced at the sky and for a second did not respond. Finally, he waved his bandaged arm. "It ain't about that, Sadie. You know I was lookin' out for you all along. Even after he threatened me. You know I wouldna give you up, no matter what. You my squeeze. Always will be. What I look like, if I can't do right by my one and only . . ."

He searched her face and saw a glimmer of what he was looking for—the fine edge of fear and sadness slowly shifting in the wake of indecision. He remained where he was, perfectly still, and dropped his voice lower.

"Soon's I got myself together, I took my life in my hands and went to meet with the father again. He said you was facin' life in prison for takin' the kid 'cross state lines. I told him you was takin' real good care of her. He relaxed a whole lot when he heard that. Wasn't so mad. We talked a lot, you know. It was hard but now he's ready to cut a deal."

"What deal?" A shade of suspicion clouded her face as she stared.

"Give him back the baby and you don't do no jail time. In fact, in fact, listen to this. He said you can even be the godmother . . ."

Sadie looked at Conroy, then gazed up into the darkening sky.

. . . Godmother? Godmother?

Her face cleared but a trace of confusion remained. She had taken care of Babygirl as if the child were her own. This was the baby she had always wanted but how much longer could she hide, how much longer could she run away, how often did she jump up and try to quiet the child when there was a noise at the door? How often had she watched the news on the broken down TV, wondering when they'd say something about a missing baby?

She looked again at Conroy's battered face and bandaged head and her heart ached. Here he was, so sick and yet willing to put his life on the line.

"You tellin' me the truth, Conroy? He really said that?"

"True as I'm sittin' here. Look, Sadie, this is too serious to bullshit about. When I told 'im how good you was with the kid, he was so happy, he said there won't be no arrest. You can see the baby anytime you want. You know, like share the kid."

He lowered his head and stared at the cracked tarring at his feet. "Otherwise, he comin' after me again, maybe finish the job this time."

She turned away again and gazed across the rooftops. The sun had dropped behind the buildings across the avenue and a red shadow spread over the roof. She positioned the baby's head on her shoulder and moved to sit next to him.

"I don't know, Conroy. I'm sorry you got beat. I'm sorry about everything. If I had known what was what, I woulda acted different. But I didn't hear from you, I didn't know nuthin'. And then I kinda . . . I mean Babygirl kinda grew on me, you know what I mean? She just grew on me . . . Here I am, twenty-six years old and I ain't never had no kids and I needed . . ."

Her face was streaked in the fading light and Conroy eased his arm around her. "I know, Sadie, I know. Don't you think on it. From here on in, it's you and me and everything gonna be all right. He promised you can see the kid. His word is his word."

He drew a deep breath and clasped his hands. "The only thing is he's one a them hard motherfuckas. Promised if this thing don't happen, he comin' after us. Take me off. Then put you in jail. Maybe for the rest of your life. Kidnappin' is serious. But we ain't got to worry about that. 'Cause we gonna do the right thing."

She was crying so hard, her shoulders were shaking. The child had fallen asleep and woke at the sound. Conroy looked at his watch as she murmured something and patted the baby back to sleep.

"You need somebody to look after you," he said softly, wiping at her tears. "You got too much on you right now. We get back together, like in old times and . . ."

She turned to face him. "What about the mother?" she whispered. "This child's real mother? Don't she have no say-so in this thing?"

Conroy shook his head. "Mama left. She and the baby's daddy wasn't makin' it too tough from the jump, so when all this came down, with the kid disappearin' and all, she couldn't take the pressure. The daddy told me she vacated and went over to her other man. So you see, the father ain't got nobody. That's why he so anxious to get a look at his daughter."

She was silent for a moment; then she held the baby away from her and whispered. "God, if I'd only known all this was gonna happen, I wouldna done—"

"Baby, you didn't know. Neither did I. I expected him to pay me them dollars he owed. Remember? Instead, he jumped bad. Why you think I come up over the roof. It was in case he was shadowin' me. I was lookin' out for you, makin' sure that nuthin' happened. And you can see everything's cool. All we got to do is follow his instructions.

"What instructions?"

He edged closer, touched her lightly behind her ear, and trailed his finger down the side of her neck. "For returnin' the kid," he whispered. Then he dropped his hand from her shoulder and tightened it around her waist. "Lemme handle everything. You too upset."

CHAPTER 33

Day 20

Marin slit the envelope open with his thumbnail and knew what it contained before he removed the letter. *No news is good news.*

On particularly bad days, when Mama Pat gathered Margaret in her arms, she had comforted her with a whisper: "No news is good news. I know my grandchild is alive. I can feel it. God is lookin' out and He got somebody special takin' care of her. God is lookin' out. We ain't heard nuthin' so no news is good news."

No news is good news.

Marin unfolded the note and read it, took a deep breath, and read it again. The message he somehow had been expecting was in his hands, yet he remained where he was, locked in the bathroom, where he read it a third time.

It was cobbled together in crude mismatched, misspelled block letters, short and to the point.

CLOK TICKING

$5000 ON VIADOC AT ST. NICH AVINUE

uNDer GREEN MAILBOX   MIDNITE FRIDAY

BABY DIe IF YOU CALL POLICE

Marin pressed the letter to his chest. His heart was pounding and his hands shook . . . *She's alive! Oh, my God. Our baby's still alive.*

The brown envelope had come in the mail addressed to him, not Mr. and Mrs. Taylor. Whoever had the baby must know there was a mother in the picture, not just a father. The thought was fleeting.

. . . Maybe they figure I'd be able to come up with the money faster than Margaret. Who knows? Who cares? Our baby is alive. Meredith is alive.

He sat on the edge of the bathtub trying to decide if he should show the note to Margaret. He read it again and decided not to. The threat of death would probably be too much for her to handle. Their child was alive and he had to get the money.

. . . It's somebody who knows me, knows my address. The newspaper never mentioned where we lived, just said it was a young couple uptown. Wasn't no pictures with the story. And it wasn't on TV or Chance or Jimmy would've told me. But it's somebody who knows me.

He thought of Eunice again but decided it wasn't her. She'd had enough to deal with with her sister.

He slipped the note in his jacket pocket, kissed Margaret and Mama Pat, and hurried out of the house.

Chance had called earlier, before the letter arrived, to tell him that Thelma had retrieved her jewelry and he had taken her to the Fat Man to celebrate. Marin had listened to Chance's excitement above the noise and music.

"Marin, I'm tellin' you, this is some pretty woman. Some pretty woman. She's a dance teacher at the Y. The cat who did this to her oughtta have his head examined."

"She found Conroy?"

"No, her cousin had set something up and put the word out. One of those 'no questions asked' kinda situations, and he walked into it. Love of money make people do crazy shit."

"Did she say anyhthing else?"

"Nada, but she's willin' to work with us. Burnt my ear tellin' me what a son of a bitch he was. Anyway, come on by. She wearin' one of the necklaces and it looks good. She'd look good in anything. I'm thinkin' of takin' dance lessons. Come on. We waitin' for you."

He walked up the hill at 145th Street wondering how to pull Chance away from Thelma and show him the letter without involving her.

. . . *Today's Wednesday. I got two days and one unemployment check. What's left in Carver is readin' near zero. Chance is the only one I know with that kind of money. He's lookin' to buy that new car with straight cash. Don't believe in owin' the Man a penny more than he have to.*

He turned north onto St. Nicholas Avenue and hurried past the Pink Angel, where singing waiters kept the club crowded every night. Sandra, the waitress, was spreading the tablecloths, preparing for the late afternoon crowd. She saw him and waved and he returned the gesture but did not slow down.

. . . *Two days. Forty-eight hours. Clyde has that kind of money too. Maybe. No. Instead of true cash, he'd want to rig a pimp roll. Tens on top and paper underneath. Then bring the high-power crew to lay in wait.*

When the deal goes down, they turn the spot into a free fire zone and light up the night.

At 155th Street, he stepped into the Fat Man. Inside it was cool and dark and the sound of Gloria Lynne on the jukebox glided softly and smoothly through the place. At the end of the bar, Chance was entertaining Thelma with incidents that happened on his route. He had his hands behind his back demonstrating how he'd once used his special cuffs on a drug addict he'd caught stealing checks out of the mailboxes and how the tenants had taught the thief a hard lesson before the cops arrived.

"You did that?" Thelma said, clapping her hand to her mouth.

"Naw. Only supplied the hardware. I'm a government employee. Ain't supposed to take the law into my own hands."

Marin heard her laugh and saw Chance smile.

Jimmy also laughed and greeted Marin with a handshake. "What's happenin'? Got a serious crease in your face. Everything all right?"

"So far. Everything's cool, Jimmy."

Chance patted him on the back, "I was just tellin' Thelma about that time I—"

He looked in Marin's face. "What's goin' on?"

Thelma glanced from one to the other and caught the signal.

"I need to see the little girls' room," she murmured. She picked up her purse and touched Chance's face. "Be back in a minute."

Jimmy moved to the other end of the counter to serve another customer. Gloria Lynne's song ended and Otis Redding's voice came on. Marin glanced toward the closed door of the ladies' room and nodded. "We need to step outside for this one. Tell Jimmy we be right back."

Outside, fast-moving silver-edged clouds were rolling in from the east and a strong wind had kicked up. Chance gripped the letter in his hands to prevent it from blowing away. A minute later, he handed it back to Marin and was silent.

He folded his arms and looked across the avenue toward the rumble of trucks and cars streaming across the viaduct. Two teenagers on rollerskates skimmed down the walkway toward Seventh Avenue. A young man and a woman with a small dog followed. He watched until they disappeared.

"Look like the stuff has hit the fan, my man. No sense wastin' time. We got to make it to the bank. It's right down the hill. Same place Dinah used to live upstairs when she wasn't on the road. We get this taken care of. When the baby's home, you figure out what to do next."

"Man, you'd do that for me?"

Chance was still gazing at the viaduct. "You my Aye Bee Cee. Don't even need to ask."

At the bank, there was a temporary delay when Chance asked for the five thousand dollars in cash.

The teller, a short brown man with a receding hairline, peered at him over the tip of his glasses. "Sir, for sums in this amount, we only issue checks."

Chance leaned close to the window. "Listen, I didn't use no check when I put it in, I ain't takin' no check when I pull it out."

He rested his elbows on the ledge, prepared to wait as the teller scratched at an invisible itch under his chin and held the withdrawal slip nearer to the light, searching for a discrepancy in the signature. "I see—"

Chance slammed the flat of his hand on the counter. "No, you don't see. Git the manager. Maybe his eyesight is better than yours."

The teller sighed and glanced beyond him. "The manager's not—"

"Don't give me that shit. Busy or not. Tell 'im to git the fuck over here."

The guard, who had been standing by the entrance, ambled over.

He looked older than the first brick that went into building the place. He squared his shoulders and laid a hand on Chance's arm.

"Now, son—"

"Excuse me . . . You my daddy?"

"Well, now that's—"

"Well now, nuthin'. My money's in here and I'm gettin' it out. Where's the damn manager?"

The lines at the other windows had paused and more eyes than necessary were staring.

"I was sayin', no need for that kind of language," the guard whispered. He was unarmed and probably retired from his regular job and wishing he had taken the day off from this one.

Chance shrugged. "Language? Maybe you're right. We don't seem to understand each other. A black face in a black neighborhood show up to transact a little serious business and y'all get all nervous. Why? Where's the damn manager? Hidin' under his desk? Tell 'im to get his ass out here and start countin' my money!"

A wood-paneled door slid open and a tall man with white hair and square rimless glasses strolled across the floor.

"Mr. Watkins? How are you? Would you care to step into my office?"

Ten minutes later, they emerged, with the manager making a show of shaking Chance's hand. "Your transaction will take a few minutes. Please have a seat and I apologize again for the misunderstanding."

Chance didn't smile but walked across the marble floor and eased into a chair next to Marin.

"I didn't know so much money could cause so much trouble," Marin said.

"Neither did I." Chance folded his arms and smiled but he was still simmering. "Chump was scared I was takin' my business to another bank. Offered me all kind of extra interest, bonds, and stuff. When I mentioned it was for a car, he tried to talk me into financin' it through the bank. Fuck 'em."

Fifteen minutes later, they pulled to the curb in front of Marin's house. The small box rested on his lap and he was suddenly nervous.

"You hold on to it till Friday, Chance."

"Naw, my man. This is your play. Besides, it's less than forty-eight hours now. Whatever move you make, I'm in your shadow. But it's your call. Give it up and get your kid. I'll be the god-daddy when you git around to celebratin'. We Aye Bee Cees, remember?"

He stared through the window and drummed his fingers against the steering wheel, fast and light. Marin thought of a pianist he'd seen at Minton's one night doing the same thing but now he looked down at the box. It was costing five thousand dollars to buy back his baby, and the finger drumming sounded different. It reflected Chance's attitude at the bank, his loud talk, belligerence, and anger. To Chance, it wasn't about the money at all but the knowledge that less than forty-eight hours would tell the tale and he was uptight. His Aye Bee Cee would be walking into something that he might not come out of. Not like the last time.

CHAPTER 34

Day 21, 3 A.M.

*A*ye. *Bee. Cees . . .*

Marin leaned back in the chair. The kitchen was dark and quiet except for the routine sounds that defined the night. He listened to the sluggish movement of the bus along Eighth Avenue and the faint vibration of the kitchen window as it passed. A small wail of a siren grew smaller with distance. Closer to the window, laughter rising from the street crackled like broken glass.

He did not count the money. It was too much. More than he had seen in his life. He had tucked the box under the bathtub and, after reading the note yet again, had placed it on top of the box.

Now he spread his hands on the empty table and squeezed his eyes shut in the dark, thinking of Benjamin.

. . . It's unscientific. Only a feeling. Turns out he was on the money. Somebody wanted Meredith for ransom. They did not take her to keep for themselves, but for ransom. Enforcer and Plug had been on the hunt for Conroy to give up that knowledge, but maybe it was Conroy himself holdin' the ace. Who am I gonna meet on the viaduct? That's where everythin' started. He had my wallet and maybe what was in it turned out to be more important than that small paycheck. Maybe he had all the info he needed to pull off something like this.

He moved from the table to the closet near the sink and retrieved the weapons from the top shelf. They felt heavy in his hands. He peered in on Margaret before he returned to the table. He spread a small towel and examined the weapons under the light. First, the Enforcer's snub-nosed .38 and then the Browning 9. Both were loaded. He spun the cylinders and emptied the chambers. Then he dismantled, cleaned, oiled, reassembled, and loaded them again.

. . . Everythin' started on that viaduct and that's where everythin' ends. Ain't gonna be no slipups. Each piece gonna be workin'.

He returned the package to the closet and folded his arms on the table to rest his head but could not sleep. The dream that usually slid through the early dawn fog now formed like a cloud in his lassitude. It eased in and he heard himself speaking to Margaret in the bedroom, softly so as not to wake her. The words came and he saw himself in his mind's eye back in the jungle holding his weapon and wondering where the children had gone and where Chance had disappeared to.

There was this guy in the unit we never talked about, Margaret. Not before. Not after. I could never tell you what happened because most of the time

I had trouble believin' it myself. So everything stayed in my head and some-times it got so crowded I wanted to scream, bang my head against a wall to try to dislodge stuff. But it never worked. Dreams are like that, you know. They come and go and come again no matter what you do. Drown yourself in drink, drugs, weed, women. It didn't matter.

Well, this guy, he was older than us and real gung ho, like in the comics—except he was serious. He was left over from Korea and still looking to make a name for himself. Claim one more piece of ribbon for his chest. But a lot of us knew, when he came to the unit, that it was about more than a ribbon.

He was lookin' for one more kill. It was in his eyes. He couldn't hide it. They'd get wide like searchlights and his lips would get tight like he just swallowed somethin' by mistake. Then a minute later, they'd get kinda puffy again when he opened his mouth. He was quick on the trigger. Hell, we all was. Had to be. It was them or us, know what I mean?

One night we out on patrol, sloggin' almost knee deep in this stuff, mos-quitoes big as my foot comin' at us like freakin' dive-bombers. Now there was many nights like this. The patrol, I mean, and we was always on edge, couldn't relax or let up. So the smallest thing set you off, you know?

We hear this little rustle in the bush and knew it wasn't a bird. A second later, we come up on four women and maybe about five kids. And they was so raggedy, look like they ain't had anything to eat in days, so they had their hands out—the kids did—but the women, they kinda knew the deal. They had their hands clasped over their heads.

Now Mr. Korea—that's what we called this gung ho guy behind his back—ordered them to line up in single file. We thought we was takin' 'em prisoners, you know, back to base. Then we saw Korea's lips shrink tight and the searchlight eyes blink on and knew shit was gonna go down. We was wonderin' what we could do. I mean, these were old women and real small kids, you know?

Anyway they was standin' there. One woman said somethin' to the kids and they dropped their hands and some started to cry. I mean it was bad. All this cryin' and the mosquitoes comin' at us and the heat cuttin' off the air so *you couldn't breathe right. Next thing we hearin' is Korea givin' the order to fire. It was Chance and me he was talkin' to. Claim he testin' the brothers to see where our loyalty lay.*

We looked at each other, then at him, and told him to fuck that loyalty shit and he could go fuck himself while he at it 'cause we wasn't gunnin' down no women and kids. It was me and Chance talkin'. We was the only two brothers in the patrol. The other two guys just stood there, paralyzed.

Then one of 'em said, "How we gonna get away with this?"

And Korea said, "Give 'em a shovel. Let 'em dig and I show you."

Well that bought us some time to figure out what the hell we were gonna do. When the grave was dug, it looked like a long deep ditch. Chance had backed away and so had the others. Korea looked at me.

"Okay, Taylor. Your buddy punked out. Look like it's your show. Let's see what you thinkin' . . ."

I looked at him and didn't move. All of a sudden, we were the only two standin' there except for the women and kids. One of 'em had picked up a kid, a baby. And she was huggin' it and holdin' out her other hand, prayin' or maybe thinkin' her hand could stop a bullet. I don't know. The others was just standin' there. Too afraid to move also. I looked at them and then at Korea.

"You got the wrong man, Sarge. I ain't doin' it."

The searchlights got brighter, blinded me. He raised his weapon and the next thing, I feel this cold steel pressing against my neck.

"It's them or you," he whispered.

He was so close, I could smell his breath like a hot wet breeze on my skin. My weapon was in my hand but I couldn't raise or lower it. Like I was in one of those dreams where you couldn't move no matter how hard you tried. I couldn't even turn my head or open my mouth.

"What you gonna do, soldier boy?"

He pressed the weapon in further. It was a .45 and felt like it weighed forty-five pounds leaning in against me.

The temperature was nearly a hundred degrees but I was freezin'. I was

freezin' but my neck was so wet, the gun kept slipping and he had to press it in tight against the bone just under my ear.

I got my mouth open wide enough to say, "I ain't doin' it, Sarge."

I heard him curse. I heard the click. And I heard the sound. I fell to my knees and fired my own weapon but he had already crumpled to the ground before me. He lay there, sprawled in the mud. When I turned around, the women and kids had melted into the bush. Like the night had just opened up and sucked 'em in.

Then all those wild sounds of the night birds and the noise of the insects suddenly shut off. Like they was in a room and somebody closed a door on 'em.

And all we could hear was our own breathin'.

"Who got 'im?" someone whispered.

Chance shrugged and holstered his weapon. The gun was smoking. I heard him say, "Beats me. I wasn't even lookin'. You guys see anything?"

No one answered and so we unrolled a tarp, each of us grabbed an edge, and we dragged Korea the two miles back to base.

Nobody spoke. It was the quietest march I'd ever been on. Everyone was thinkin' that they knew. Or thought they knew.

It was so dark, it seemed like the stars had fallen out of the sky. And too dark for a positive ID but that didn't stop my thoughts from spinnin' out of my head. For Korea, the decision had been made that it was gonna be him or me. He got what he got and even as I carried his body, I wasn't thinkin' about him anymore. My mind was on those kids.

A half mile from base, we walked into an ambush. Had to shoot our way out. We lit up the night and the last thing I felt was my leg giving out from under me. I'd gotten it in the back and didn't even know it. I woke up in the hospital and wondered about those kids. I never told you that, Margaret, but since our baby disappeared, I think about them all the time. I wonder where they ran to. They were dirty, hungry, scared. In my sleep, I hear them crying. And I wonder where they are.

CHAPTER 35

Day 21

"So why we gotta dress up a doll? I thought we was meetin' with the father. We give back Babygirl, he give you the money he owe, and I get to see her anytime I want. Y'all made the deal. What's goin' on?"

Sadie sat on the edge of her bed watching Conroy fit a pink knitted cap on the doll's head and then wrap it in several blankets.

"Insurance, Sadie. This is insurance in case the motherfucka try to pull a fast one. He supposed to put

239

the package under that green mailbox. You place this doll there and pick up the money. I check it to see if it's for real and then I give you the baby to take to him. Okay?"

She fanned her fingers along the edge of the bedspread, nodding slowly, trying to make up her mind about something she did not fully grasp. "Suppose he want to see the child first? I can't show him no make-believe. Then what? What do I do?"

"Nuthin' 'cause he ain't gonna ask. It'll be midnight. Dark. He knows he don't get the kid until I get the money in my hands. That's the deal. You play your part and everything'll be fine."

Before she could ask another question, he strode out of the room and closed himself in the bathroom. Too many questions were coming at him too fast, tripping his last nerve.

Last night he had gotten no sleep. Now he leaned on the basin and stared at the face in the mirror. The reflection resembled that of an old man outslicked, outgunned, and outmaneuvered. Done in by all the misfired schemes in a misspent life. His eyes were blood red and the scar above his eyelid snaked in a white line along his forehead and disappeared in his hairline. He looked at the newer scars, a roadmap of welts and bumps that made him look even older.

He was tired but convinced himself that he did his best thinking just before dawn, and this plan was going to work.

Last night, he had lain on the sofa listening to the sound of the baby in the bedroom. He heard the child cough, cry, drink from the bottle Sadie had warmed, and heard the silence that filled the room when the baby fell asleep.

He turned away from the mirror and sat on the edge of the tub trying to get a handle on the impressions spinning through his head.

. . . This kid's alive. Because of her father, my brother is dead. Tito no longer here to tell me how to make life work.

He lit a cigarette and watched the tip glow in the dim light. The bathroom was small and dark and the tub had a large gray ring inside. The basin held a small mound of diapers. He looked at the thin towel and the small facecloth printed with smiley faces draped over the rack.

Once the money is in my hand, I throw in a bonus. Take care of the kid the same way her pop took care of Tito. Leave Sadie in the middle, wild and cryin', runnin' interference. She ain't wanted to give the kid up in the first place. This way, nobody gits it. While everybody scramblin' around, I cut down the stairs to Eighth Avenue. Always a cab around there. Hop one and head for the airport, straight, no chaser. Git even for Tito and fuck everything else. Fuck Savoy, too.

He glanced in the mirror again and tried to smile.

And I'll have new dollars, new name, new rags, everything. I'll show 'em who got the last word. Sissy-steppin' motherfucka think he dump my brother and git away. Eye for an eye. He gonna know how it feel to fuck up somebody's life.

He yawned wide and caught a whiff of his breath, heavy with the stale residue of cigarettes and fatigue.

He had remained awake the entire night, listening for the light sound of footsteps, the slow turn of the lock, ready to spring if Sadie had changed her mind and tried to sneak the baby out.

He spoke to the image. "Fuck it. This gonna work."

CHAPTER 36

Day 21

Friday morning dawned gray and wet. Marin sat at the kitchen table thinking maybe he should wrap the money in plastic before he took it to the viaduct. Was Conroy working alone? A soggy, too-heavy package might make the man suspicious and blow everything.

He thought of the guns and was glad he'd moved them from the closet, put them under the tub with the money. Couldn't afford any last-minute snags. This had to go off without a hitch.

Margaret sat across from him sipping from her third cup of coffee. She averted her gaze when he looked at her.

"Come on now. What's the matter?"

She put her cup down and leaned her elbows on the table. Her face was reddish brown in the dim light and her eyes were wide and flecked with tints of hazel.

"Last night, you didn't sleep at all," she said. "I turned over and heard you in the kitchen. Moving from the bathroom to the kitchen and back again. You all right?"

Marin looked at her, surprised. "I'm okay. Just a little—"

"I think I know what you're gonna say, Marin. I'm tired also. Real tired. I wish . . . No. I don't wish anymore. I want this whole thing—this waiting and not knowing to be over. I want us to find out once and for all—about Meredith."

She rose from the table and stood by the window, gazing out. Clouds were moving to the west and taking what was left of the rain with them. The sky emerged, clean and ice blue, and streaks of sunlight reflected pale pink against the windows across the avenue.

She leaned against the sink and Marin studied the straight line of her spine, the curve of her hips, and the slant of her shoulders in the light. Her hair was tied in a knot at the nape of her neck and her housedress was fastened tightly around her waist. She was frowning when she turned to face him.

"We're so focused on the baby," she said. "I think of her twenty-four hours a day and I know you do also. Lately, I've been feeling like everything has drained out of us—our energy, our hopes, our—"

"No. No!" He held up his hand and she stopped when she saw his expression. She moved to the table, took his hand, and held it tightly against her chest.

"I'm sorry. I didn't mean it the way it came out," she whispered. "I love you. I always will. But I just need to—know something. Anything. I'm trying to be strong. But I'm not like you. I wonder all the time how much more I can take. Whether I can go on like this."

He felt the pulse of her heart beating against his palm. He took her hands and pressed them to his mouth and did not want to let go. The loss of Meredith was pulling her away from him. He could feel it. What had happened to them? To their marriage?

This thing that had come on them should have brought them closer. In the beginning, in those first few days, it had. Then she had suddenly pulled away to live in a place inside herself. Her thoughts were her own. Later, she had seemed to come back, to reconnect. But she wasn't her old self. She was strange and new. A butterfly emerging from a cocoon. Changed. Quick to anger if her questions went unanswered. She was asking again and he still could not answer. Too much was riding on it. What if Meredith was returned to them dead? What if the whole thing turned out be a hoax and she was not returned at all?

He eased the chair away from the table and pulled Margaret into his lap. Her head rested on his shoulder and he listened to the sound of her breathing. He closed his eyes, and images he couldn't speak about spun through his head. He saw the long narrow walkway that would lead him up to the viaduct at midnight. The green mailbox under which he would put the money, then move a short distance away to watch as the baby was placed there in exchange. Margaret moved in his lap but he tried not to open his eyes. He wanted to reach the point where the baby would finally be in his arms, and Margaret's face would be glowing. She moved again, trying to find a comfortable place. He held her to him and the image vanished.

CHAPTER 37

Day 21, Evening

"You haven't touched a thing on your plate," Mama Pat said. "Probably all those cigarettes you been smokin' all day. Never seen anybody go through two packs so fast."

Marin stubbed the last cigarette out. "Everything looked so good but I'm not really hungry. I'm sorry."

"That's all right. I get them days too."

"We all do," Naomi said. She was standing at the sink washing the dishes, and he wondered if he should have at least confided in her. What if something went wrong and he didn't make it back . . .

He looked up and caught Margaret's gaze. She was silent but her eyes held a cool intelligence that told him not to worry; that everything, whatever it was, was going to be all right.

At nine o'clock, Mama Pat and Naomi left. At ten, Margaret was already in bed. He peeked into the room. A soft breeze flowed through the window, ruffling the curtains. "I'm out of smokes, baby. Be back in a while."

"Don't stay too long," she whispered, already half asleep.

He stepped into the room, kissed her forehead, and turned on the small lamp on the night table. The dim light bathed her face in a vapory halo. "Keep my spot warm," he said.

In the bathroom, he placed the weapons under his shirt and hefted the package in the crook of his arm. Five thousand in hundred dollar bills was not heavy. He glanced in the mirror. The shirt hung straight and smooth, no bulges, and the package, wrapped in plastic, looked ordinary enough.

In the hall, his footfalls echoed softly on the marble steps.

. . . This is it. If the joker's dealing a bad deck, he'll never play again.

The night air against his face was crisp and cool enough to steady him. He walked uptown past the Dunbar Apartments and detoured onto Macombs Place. At Seventh Avenue, he strolled past the Flash Inn, where a small wedding reception was taking place. Two men in formal dress stood at the curb gazing at the passing traffic. Both were smoking and one held a drink in his hand. Their talk floated above the hum of traffic and Marin caught bits of conversation as he passed: "First time I met the cat, I peeped his hole card. He ain't never been cool with his shit. Now he married? That ain't hardly goin' nowhere."

The second man shrugged and raised his glass to his mouth. "Well, from what I see, the bride ain't no dummy. Here's hopin' she don't do him in when she figures it all out."

The viaduct was deserted except for a few cars moving infrequently along the roadway. Marin checked his watch for the third time and walked faster even though he knew he was early. Halfway up the steep incline he glanced down on Eighth Avenue. A lighted ribbon of traffic flowed in an unbroken line to 110th Street. Dots of light blinked from tenement roofs, and he guessed that folks were lounging under the stars on chairs and blankets, trying to catch the breeze, as he and Margaret often did.

He passed the stairs leading ten flights down to Eighth Avenue. One of the boards usually nailed across the entrance still had not been replaced and he looked at the top step, splintered and rotted away.

. . . *Worse than the last time. Somebody else ease up here and get taken off before it's fixed. This was in some white neighborhood, it woulda been fixed long time ago. They woulda—*

A shadow slipped into view at the far end of the viaduct, cutting into his reverie. The person, a woman, walked in small steps toward the mailbox but did not stop. He quickened his pace but by the time he reached St. Nicholas Avenue, she had disappeared.

He looked across the street. The lights of the Fat Man spread like a layer of white powder over the pavement but the glow reached only as far as the curb. The avenue itself was deserted, except for a lone bike rider cruising several blocks away.

Where had the woman gone? Had she ducked into one of the buildings?

He retraced his steps and placed the package under the mailbox, then walked diagonally across the street from the bar to stand in the shadow of a hundred-year-old oak a few feet from the corner. From his vantage point, he could view the avenue and the whole of the viaduct.

He checked his watch again. A minute past midnight, he spotted a woman again. He studied her walk and knew it was the same one. He stepped farther into the shadows and held his breath as she bent to pick up the package. She hugged it to her and glanced around before hurrying down the walkway. In the distance, a man approached carrying a wrapped bundle and Marin's breath caught in his throat.

He's got Meredith.

He stepped away from the tree and eased his hand under his shirt. The .38 felt cool in his palm.

The woman had hurried toward the man. When she reached him, he snatched at the plastic package, ripping it open with one hand. Then he held a stack of dollars close to his face as if to breathe in the smell of all the good things destined to come his way. He opened his mouth and his laughter drifted on the wind.

Then he said something and the woman stepped back, her hands to her face. A second later, she was struggling, trying to pull the bundled child from his arms. The voices, indecipherable at first, grew loud.

"Bitch! Lemme go. I know what I'm doin'!"

"But that's not what you said you was gonna do! Why you didn't bring the doll for me to leave? Ohhh! You told me we was gonna—"

"Fuck you! Don't tell me what I said!"

She had her hands around his neck and almost appeared to be dancing when Marin sneaked up. He came up on them without a word and was a few feet away when the man reached out and brought his fist down with the force of a hammer on the woman's forehead. She staggered back, then fell to the ground screaming. When he turned around, Marin had his pistol in his face.

"You got the money. Now let go of the baby, Conroy. Just hand her over nice and easy and nobody gets hurt!"

"What? How you know my name?" He stood wide-legged, hugging the baby, and Marin could hear the muffled crying.

"Give me the baby! Give her up! That was the deal!"

Conroy held the baby close to his chest and backed away. "It wasn't supposed to be this way, but okay, motherfucka. Think you got the upper hand. Go 'head. Take your best shot. First bullet gits the kid."

"No!" The scream came out of the night as Sadie threw herself against Marin. "No. No. That's not what you promised."

She fell into him hard, staggering him. In that half second, Conroy stepped back to lean near the railing.

"You think you on top, motherfucka? Drop the heat or your kid goes."

He balanced the child on the railing, ready to let go. Marin dropped the gun.

"Now kick it over here."

Marin kicked it away but Sadie, still crouched on the ground, scrambled fast and snatched it up.

"Conroy, you lied! Give me back my baby, you son of a bitch . . ." She was on her knees, aiming the gun at Conroy. Blood streamed from her mouth and her eyes were lit as if an explosion had gone off behind her head. Marin had his hands in the air, watching her, watching Conroy, watching for the next move.

Sadie held her arms rigid in front of her, steadying the weapon with both hands. "Give her to me, I said."

Conroy looked surprised, then he frowned. He had the plastic bag tucked under his arm and he balanced the baby on the railing. "Okay, okay, Sadie. Put the piece down. You forget we in this together. What goes down with me goes down for you too. Put the piece down."

But she remained in the crouch and her arms did not waver. Marin backed away to ease toward Conroy. He was within arm's reach when Sadie said. "Conroy, we was supposed to leave the doll. This ain't what you promised. And you said I could see the baby if I gave her up. You lied, didn't you."

Then she swung the gun toward Marin. "Both of you lied. Y'all lied to me."

She was shouting and pointing the gun first at Marin, then at

Conroy, trying to decide whom to hit first. Marin knew if she squeezed the trigger, the baby would be gone before he or Conroy hit the ground.

He extended both hands toward her. "Look . . . Sadie. No. I didn't lie. You can see the baby anytime you want. Anytime. Just put the gun down. You might hurt her. And that's not what you want."

Her eyes were wide when she looked at him, but she said nothing.

"It's gonna be all right," Marin said. "I promise you."

"I been promised too many things too many times," she whispered, staring at Conroy. "This is one time too many."

"Come on, Sadie. Do as he says. And things won't be so hard on you. He know what he talkin' about," Conroy said. He eyed her with a cool detachment. The baby was still balanced on the railing as he spoke, as if he were holding a package of nondescript goods, to be discarded without a thought once its utility ended.

Marin's legs trembled and his heart beat like a trip-hammer, threatening to seize up within him.

Sadie remained silent. She looked up at the sky, then at Conroy and seemed to deflate as she blew out a breath.

"Conroy if you—"

She placed the gun on the sidewalk. Conroy shifted the baby in his arms to reach for it and Marin lunged. He grabbed the child as Conroy dove for the weapon. Marin drew the Browning from under his shirt and fired. The force of the bullet ripped the weapon from Conroy's hand and he lay on the ground howling.

The baby's screams could be heard above everything as Conroy scrambled to his feet and tried to run for the stairs.

"I ain't doin' no time, motherfucka! I ain't doin' no time! This shit is all on her!"

Marin aimed again and shot him in the leg. Conroy dropped the plastic bag and crawled on his stomach, trying to make it to the stairs. The trail of blood resembled a smear of ink in the dim light, and

Marin watched silently, knowing if Conroy made it to the exit, he would break through the rotted step to sail ten stories out of his life.

He waited and held tightly to the baby in one hand and felt the heat of the smoking weapon in the other.

A few feet from the exit, Conroy rolled over on his back and lay still.

The noise had been frightening and the baby cried louder, startling Marin. He put the gun in his waistband and shifted the child in his arms. "Meredith. Meredith. It's all right. It's all right."

He pulled away the blanket and stared at her. She smelled of milk and baby powder, and her face was pinched with fright. She squirmed and kicked and each movement caused Marin's heart to strike against his chest like a ball in a shaken box.

He heard Sadie call to him. "Just hold . . . her head, mister." She knelt on the ground with her face against the guardrail. Her hands were clasped to her waist and she stared vacantly at the ribbon of traffic on the avenue below. The damaged gun lay a few feet away. When she spoke again, her voice was so soft, it seemed not to belong to her.

"Just . . . hold her head close to you," she whispered. "Tell her you love her and she get calm. She be all right."

A light wind rose and blew her hair out of her swollen face. Her mouth was open and her teeth were stained red. Marin moved quickly to kneel beside her. "Sadie. Sadie." He pressed his handkerchief against her face. "Everything's gonna be all right."

EPILOGUE

"You should've just let him bleed to death. Save the
state a fortune," sighed Benjamin. He sat at the
kitchen table squeezing a slice of lemon into his iced
tea. His collarless shirt was open at the throat and his
straw hat rested on his knee. He spoke in a whisper,
aware that Margaret was in the next room with the
baby and Mama Pat and Naomi, and that the door
was ajar. Their laughter and excitement floated above
the baby's murmur.

Marin lounged in the chair across from Benjamin. The kitchen fan was on high speed and still not doing its job.

"I know what you mean. Personally, I would've let him lay but my backup was hangin' in the Fat Man and we had our stuff timed to the second. The plan was if I didn't show with the baby in fifteen minutes, he was to drop a dime. That's what he did and the ambulance got there faster than I could blink.

"Besides, I had my hands full. When Sadie realized that she wouldn't be seeing the baby anymore, she went around the bend. I mean she went out of it. Screamin' that her life was over and threatenin' to kill herself. She had been completely centered around Meredith. The baby had been taken from her and she had nuthin' else to live for. It was all I could do to hold on to her to keep her from jumpin', and at the same time not let go of the baby.

"Before it was all over, there were three ambulances and more cops on the scene than I wanted to count. They wanted to take Meredith too. To be examined, they said, but no way was anybody gettin' hold of my child again. No way. They would've had to kill me first."

He put his hand to his head. "I'm damn glad this is over. All over. It's been . . ."

He said no more. In the silence they listened to the baby's sounds and to Margaret's quiet laughter.

Since they had refused to take the child to the hospital, the administrator, mindful of the pending lawsuit, had obliged by sending a pediatrician, a nurse, and a social worker to the house in the middle of the night.

The examination had lasted two hours and then they weighed Meredith on a portable scale.

"This baby was well cared for," the doctor said. "There're no bruises, scars, broken bones, neurological problems or signs of malnutrition. She's fine and very healthy considering all she's been through."

The nurse had wrapped the baby and handed her to Margaret as the social worker took in the condition of the apartment and nodded.

They had left at 3 A.M., and Marin spent the next hour reassembling the crib. They were still awake when Mama Pat and Naomi rushed in, breathless, to wake the child and examine her again to determine if she was indeed the child and that she was in one piece.

"The birthmark, Mama Pat. Look at the birthmark," Marin had said, barely able keep his eyes open.

At 5 A.M. Benjamin knocked on the door and Margaret was glad to see him. "What's gonna happen to Sadie?" she asked. "She took care of my baby. Doesn't that count for something? What's gonna happen to her?"

"My guess," Benjamin said, "is that she'll stay in the hospital for a while and then be reevaluated to determine if she's competent to stand trial, you know, participate in her own defense.

"Either way, I can't see her doing any time. If it goes to trial, the defense will stack the jury with enough women who have known someone like Conroy once or twice in their lives. They won't put her away.

"As for Conroy himself, the disaster master with a sheet longer than Scott's tissue—once he's patched up enough to hobble before the bench, he's looking at lifetime rent-free accommodations with a wonderful upstate view."

Somewhat satisfied, Margaret returned to the bedroom. Benjamin waited, then drained his glass and looked at his watch. "Let's take a walk. We got to talk."

The early morning fog had burned off and the sun broke through, painting the storefronts along Eighth Avenue a fiery ocher, a forecast of a midday temperature of at least ninety.

257

They strolled along the avenue toward Bradhurst Park and at 145th Street stood near the wrought-iron gates of the Colonial Pool watching the early morning swimmers take advantage of the freebie.

A maintenance worker finished skimming a scatter of leaves from the water, and the pool, clear of debris, reflected the scud of pink-edged clouds overhead. Morning traffic roared along the wide avenue and people rushed up the hill to catch the A train.

"There's a little matter we need to clear up," Benjamin said, turning away from the pool. "May as well take care of it now, off the record. This way I close the book before somebody else decides it should be on the record."

"A little matter like what?"

"Small stuff. Like where'd you come by all that artillery you were packing?"

Marin gazed at a child diving into the pool. The girl cut the water without breaking a wave.

"That .38 belonged to Conroy, not to me."

"Okay, so what about the Browning 9?"

"I found it."

Benjamin closed his eyes and pinched the skin above his nose as if to clear his sinuses. "Standard," he said, more to himself than to Marin.

Marin looked at him. "Standard what?"

"Standard response. After an incident, every time I ask, that's the answer. 'Found it.' At that rate, everybody in Harlem should be tripping over a weapon every time they step out the house. Come on, man. You can do better than that."

Marin shook his head. "No I can't. I found it and that's the word. Want me to show you the spot?"

Benjamin sighed and tried a different tack. "I want to know why you didn't bother to turn it in?"

Marin tapped a finger to his chest. "After what happened to me? Turn it in? Is that a trick question?"

Benjamin gazed at the water again and decided to change the subject. He would bring it up again if circumstances warranted.

"The DEA took down a big-time operation last night. No, you wouldn't know that. You haven't had time for the papers yet and last night you were too wrapped up in your own stuff.

"But when you read it, don't be surprised. Big investigation in the works, as usual. Paper jumped all over the fact that my partner was inside that house. Found with nothing on and a bullet to the brain. Took the easy way out as they closed in."

He stopped talking and they moved away from the iron gate and the cool light on the water. On Eighth Avenue, away from the pool, the air felt thick and Marin wanted nothing more than to go home and stand under the shower and feel all the stress and strain of the last weeks float away. And he wanted to hold Meredith in his arms and listen to all her small sounds, catch and remember them.

They strolled past Miss Adelaide's, where only one seat was occupied. She waved them in and they took a table by the window directly under the large wood-bladed fan.

Benjamin studied the menu as he spoke. "This is strictly off the record, Taylor, but what were you doing scoping Savoy's place?"

"I was trackin' a rumor that two of his heavyweights, Fireplug and Enforcer, might have had some inside knowledge about my baby."

"Find anything?"

"Didn't have time. They got taken off too fast. Less than twenty-four hours. How'd that happen?"

"As far as we can figure from the tapes, it happened like this. Savoy always demanded complete loyalty. In his line of work, I suppose he had to. He had Leahy tap their phones and heard the talk and he figured he'd better get them before they did him. He gave the order and Leahy obliged. Took care of Enforcer and set up Plug to get taken out on a hummer.

"In that game, nobody trusts their own shadow. Everyone's got to watch their back and at the same time keep an eye on the next man who's got his hand in the next pocket. A no-win situation but they couldn't see beyond the dollars.

"I was put in the street to see if Leahy would try to turn me, but he was too deep in his special thing. We left it to the DEA to make the move; then we joined in. Savoy is doing his bird act, lookin' for leniency, but he can forget it. He had those underage girls in there."

Benjamin studied the menu for several minutes before deciding on a deluxe platter of fried red snapper, fish cakes, broiled shrimp, buttered grits, a double order of biscuits, and a large iced tea. He placed the menu on the table and rested his elbows on it. He caught Marin's stare.

"Did you leave anything out?" Marin asked.

Benjamin leaned back in his chair, freeing up the menu.

"I work hard," he answered. "Got to maintain optimum fighting strength."

Miss Adelaide approached and Marin sighed and ordered a cup of coffee. He knew Margaret and Mama Pat and Naomi were by now in the kitchen with the pots and pans probably falling off the stove. Then again, maybe not. They'd be too busy with the baby. He canceled the coffee, scanned the menu again, and ordered a sensible breakfast.

ABOUT THE AUTHOR

Grace F. Edwards was born and raised in Harlem and now lives in Brooklyn. She is a member of the Harlem Writers Guild and teaches creative writing at Marymount Manhattan College. She is the author of five other novels.